I SHOULD HAVE SOLD PETUNIAS

Don Honig

A JOVE/HBJ BOOK

Copyright © 1977 by Don Honig

All rights reserved. No part of this publication may be reproduced or transmitted in any form or by any means, electronic or mechanical, including photocopy, recording, or any information storage and retrieval system, without permission of the author.

First Jove/HBJ edition published September 1977

Library of Congress Catalog Card Number: 77-77251

Printed in the United States of America

Jove/HBJ books are published by Jove Publications, Inc. (Harcourt Brace Jovanovich), 757 Third Avenue, New York, N.Y. 10017

After you've been around awhile you get to know a little something about men...

"I've learned to tell when they're in love, when they've changed their minds about it, when they're horny, when they've got real trouble, and almost anything else you want to think of. *Including when they want to kill you.*"

Terry wasn't really a bad girl . . . she just got involved with the wrong guys. Like Ned. Ten minutes after she met him, he offered her a delicious summer in the Hamptons . . . free. Then a plush apartment on New York's Upper East Side. Next came Charley. He took her to fancy restaurants and to Vegas for weekends.

So she never asked any questions, like where they got all the cash, or why they never discussed business in front of her . . . But when the *cops* started asking her questions, things began to change. And the day Charley decided she had to be killed, Terry knew her lifestyle was definitely not going to remain a bed of roses!

To
Edward Bartley

Chapter One

After you've been around awhile you get to know a little something about men. It isn't the most heartwarming knowledge in the world. But men don't hide their thoughts and feelings from women as much as they do from other men; they probably don't think we're that interested, and most of the time we're not. But that doesn't mean we don't know about them. I've learned to tell when they're in love, when they've changed their minds about it, when they're horny, when they've got real trouble, and almost anything else you want to think of. Including when they want to kill you.

This last piece of knowledge came to me sideways, so to speak; that is, I wasn't really looking for it. (I should have been looking for it, I suppose, but I'm a trusting soul—you know, the sort of person who went out of style two hundred years ago.) It isn't always crucial to know when a guy's in love, or when he's horny, or when he's got problems; most of it's just an extra clutter in your head. But you can't overemphasize the importance of knowing when a guy wants to kill you. Or as it was in my case, two guys.

How do you know? Well, you do. It's the same kind of knowing as when you feel a change coming in the weather. In this case it was the immediate atmosphere that was changing and it was the men who were changing it. You can know this very clearly when you're riding in a car with them, when one is driving and the other is sitting in the back seat and neither one of them is saying a word and you're being driven out to the country along back roads where you have no business being, where you never see a house or another car or a light or anything—the kind of neighborhood that probably doesn't even have a ZIP code.

It's suspicion that finally helps sharpen you up, but even that didn't begin to come awake until after we had crossed the George Washington Bridge.

"Why are we going to Jersey?"

"That's where Charley wants to see you," Mac said. He was the driver. I looked at him as he said it: his chin was angled out a bit and an outside light was just passing over his leering teeth. He wasn't a very nice-looking lout under any circumstances, but at that moment he looked worse than ever. I guess I can't imagine a hired gun being anything but unpleasant-looking; I know that all the ones I've met have had eyes like colored glass and faces that seemed pained by laughter, theirs or anybody else's.

"What's Charley doing in Jersey?" I asked. Charley lived on Long Island, hung around mostly in New York, made his visits to Vegas and Miami and Nassau, but never Jersey. I'd never heard of him going to Jersey for anything.

"I don't know," Mac said.

I believed him. His kind made a special effort not to know, as if knowledge of any kind was dangerous or unnecessary, some kind of heavy baggage they didn't feel it was worth carrying. All they knew was to do what they were told. They didn't even want to *think*. What a breed. I think there must be a farm somewhere up around the North Pole where they grow these guys.

Big Stoney in the back seat ran true to his name—he didn't say a word. Just sitting there, hat brim level with his eyes, coat collar up, hands in his pockets: in the shadows, Big Stoney was always in the shadows. He moved around with the grace and personality of somebody who had been carved out of granite. He was big and moronic and I always thought of him as Mr. I. Queless. I'd heard he'd loused up a contract in Kansas City a few years before when his gun jammed and that he was lucky to still be a member of the club.

"When did you talk to him?" I asked Mac.

"Who?" he asked.

"Charley."

"This morning."

"What did he say?"

"He said pick up Terry."

"What else?" I asked.

"He said he wants to see you in Jersey."

No sense asking why. Even if the fink knew he wouldn't tell. But any way you looked at it, it was a hell of a thing, being at their beck and call like that. Just because they paid your rent and gave you spending money and kept you out of the cold in the winter and the warm in the summer, did it mean they held this goddamned mortgage on your life? I guess it did. And anyway, you never took a chance on finding out; what I mean is, you never said no to them. One of the great unknowns in world history is what would happen if one of their broads ever said no to them. But I knew I wasn't the one for finding out; let somebody else handle that job of original research.

I had been sitting in my apartment reading a book (trying to improve my mind, like Charley said I should), thinking about a whole lot of things (I always think about something else when I read a book) when these two products of the North Pole breeding farm came knocking on the door. Charley wanted me. That was the greeting. Not hello, not how are you, not even go to hell. And behind Mac was Big Stoney, six and a half feet and a couple of hundred pounds of unrefined muscle, carrying a valise, and I thought at first he was coming to spend the night, which was scary as hell. I couldn't imagine going to bed with a lump like that; he impressed me as the kind of guy who stared you right in the eye while he was screwing. But it's been known to happen for the boss to get tired of his girl and give her away. That's the beginning of the end. You get passed along the line until you're going down for some triple-chinned tub of blubber who's taking numbers in the back room of a candy store in Queens. But I knew all that was still a long way off (if I ever permitted it to happen), because only last week Charley said I was the best piece he'd ever had, that I had some class too, and that he was never ashamed of me when I opened my mouth (we laughed at that because of the double meaning).

Anyway, they were in such a hurry I didn't even have time to powder my nose, which ticked me off because Charley always liked me to be glamorous.

After we crossed the George Washington Bridge we began riding along the Palisades. Below was a pretty nasty drop through rocks and trees straight down to the water, which was as dark as the inside of a glove. Across the Hudson you could see the lights of upper Manhattan and then the Bronx, as we went riding along. On our side of the river there was nothing, only us, our headlights picking up endless curving sweeps of trees as we followed the winding road.

Then we cut away from the river and began following some back roads. We passed through little towns that were fast asleep, zipping under yellow blinker lights, passing an occasional crossroads where there was a grocery store with a wooden porch or a closed gas station with a night light burning in the office.

Something began to bother me. I couldn't quite put my finger on it, but there was something—a little bell—pinging away in a corner of my mind. There were things that we—the girls—knew about but didn't know about. Things that the boys sometimes did when they weren't sitting ringside with us at a big fight or up front at the reserved tables of the fancy night spots. You find out without wanting to, hearing when you're not listening. Rides out into the boondocks, and then a punctured body turning up in the woods someplace or floating in the water. Sometimes they want them to be found, one of the girls told me once. Like to send out a warning to teach a lesson to somebody else.

But I had a clear conscience. Right?

I glanced at Mac. His eyes were fixed straight ahead on the road, his face blank as snow. And behind me I could feel Big Stoney sitting there like he'd been dropped into that seat from five thousand feet. What was he carrying that suitcase for? Suddenly I had visions of my sexy little body being carved up and put in there piece by piece like a birthday present for somebody. I had the damnedest wish then. I wanted to call my father. Jesus Christ, of all people. We hadn't spoken in a couple of years and he would probably hang up the minute he heard my voice. Then all of a sudden I was more worried about something else—I didn't want to just disappear, like a star dropping out of the sky when nobody is looking. If they were going to do something to me, then I wanted somebody—my mother, some friends, somebody, anybody—to know I was gone.

Christ, hey, this was serious. Of all the dumb things— what the hell was this? Charley said we'd be going to Vegas next week. And what about Miami this winter? And what about that TV special I wanted to catch tomorrow night? And I wanted to finish that book.

The stupidest things. I was thinking the stupidest things.

We'd laugh later. I'd tell Charley, "Hey, Big Man, you know what I was thinking on the way up?" He'd laugh. He had this big chesty laugh—you could hear all the phlegm swirling around in his chest. "Whatsamatter, Terry? You got a guilty conscience or something?" Ha-ha-ha-ha-ha.

Then I had to go to the bathroom. All of a sudden there it was, roaring in my kidneys like a dam had burst. I was all filled up. I pressed my knees together as hard as I could. I wanted to ask Mac to stop someplace but I was afraid to. It was as if they'd say, "What, you're still here? Jeez, we forgot about you." Leave well enough alone.

There was nothing now, less than nothing; just the headlights picking up a little road that was snaking through the trees. There were no lights, no houses, no people, no anything—just me and my two goons.

Then I found my voice.

"Mac, how far is this?"

"Not far," he said.

"What does Charley want? Do you know?"

"Charley?" he said. "He wants to see you in Jersey."

"You son of a bitch!" I screamed, suddenly remembering, as the pinging in the back of my mind became a loud bell, gonging away like doomsday. Mac laughed and reached down and turned on the radio, very loud, and all of a sudden there was a blaring of rock music that sounded positively horrible. Why did he put on the radio then and there? I knew damned well why, because that monster in the back had moved forward out of the shadows; I saw him out of the corner of my eye, and I got scared, so damned scared.

I turned around and saw him; he was still moving forward, those big squared-out shoulders advancing like a wall, no-faced under the hat brim, coat collar up ... and the gun in his hand, lining me up nice and neat. It was horrible, seeing that thing so close, the end of the barrel like an evil eye staring at me.

I threw up my hand and slapped at the gun and it went off with the damnedest explosion, so loud, so sudden, so insane I thought the car was going to go to pieces from it. The explosion, so close to my ear, filled my head with a roar so that I couldn't hear anything, and I fell sideways in my seat, certain that I was dead, and amazed that I was thinking it, as if my body had died and my head didn't know about it yet but would in another second or so. I was dead; I was thinking that, clearly and calmly, as I tumbled around in the seat. The explosion was still filling the car, the roar was still in my head, and I was dead—all of that in the splittest of split seconds. Everything seemed to have come apart in so many pieces that it would take forever and then some to put it all together again. It was all flying around—the noise and the darkness, and all the fears I'd been building up—everything released and shrieking like burning witches.

And then as I fell back against the door I saw Mac, and he was doing the damnedest thing. He wasn't holding the wheel anymore, he was sort of crunched up in the corner, half twisted around, one foot raised up in the air, and on his face was an expression of the most horrified amazement. His eyes were glaring and his mouth was open like it was trying to shape the letter O.

The car was still running, crazy fast, with nobody holding the wheel. I covered my face with my hands as I felt myself sliding off the seat, and as I went I could see Big Stoney looming over me, a hat and a coat collar and those terrifically wide shoulders, rising out of the dark. I glanced again for a second at Mac; he was still the same way, the expression of pain and horror, the one foot raised, the empty wheel in front of him. Then I looked back to Big Stoney; he was halfway to his feet now, like some giant ghost shaping itself as it came out of the ground, still with no face, only a mass of shadows and iron clothing.

And then the next thing I knew there was this wild jolting and a sound like metal grinding itself to pieces. I sank to the floor, under the dashboard and saw Big Stoney coming hurtling forward like he'd been shot out of a cannon. He went passing over me as straight and stiff as a board. I saw his chin, and then the tightly drawn belt of his trench coat and then the tips of his shoes, and there was this terrible mangling of glass and he was gone, and then the car was doing something. It felt like we were going off the edge of a cliff. The car seemed to be out in thin air for a second, touching nothing, not having any weight; but then there was more tearing and grinding and another terrific jolting and we came down with a thud and I could see Mac leaving his seat now and come flopping toward me. He was dropping straight down on me and I knew the car must have turned over. The next thing I knew his hair was in my face and I was screaming.

Then there was nothing—no noise, no motion—absolutely nothing, except I was pinned down by a dead man, another man was completely gone, and the windshield looked like it had been blasted out by a bomb.

Chapter Two

Three years ago on the hot white sands of the Hamptons, I was lying next to the bluest blue water you ever saw, under the bluest blue sky: two blue mirrors reflecting each other. My friend Denise had said to me the previous Thursday, "What are we doing this weekend?" I suggested we go out to the Hamptons. I'd heard this was the glamorous, swinging, "in" place. I needed some glamour and swinging. Life in the Bronx, especially in the summer (and especially in the winter, fall, and spring, too), is not very exciting. Depressing, in fact, would be one of the livelier words for it.

So we pooled our resources, rented a car, and drove out to the Hamptons on a steamy Friday night. It was a great trip. The car's air-conditioning broke down, the traffic stayed glued together the whole time, and when we finally got out there it was almost midnight and we were lucky to get a motel room. To top it off the guy behind the desk, a young baldy with a paunch, said he'd let us have the room for free if we all slept together in one big bed.

"No go," I told him. "Me and my friend are in love with each other."

"What'd you tell him that for?" Denise said as we walked to the room.

"It's the swinging Hamptons," I said, looking up through the warm black night at the stars that never shine over the Bronx. I had this wild feeling that it was going to be the greatest weekend ever. (How could it miss, with the send-off my mother had given me? While I was packing my bag for the weekend she stood in the doorway, hands on hips, her face a disapproving scowl. "One thing," she said in that grim growl-of-a-lion voice of hers. "Don't get pregnant.")

"Listen," I told Denise when we were inside the room, "if we pick up guys tomorrow we go our separate ways—agreed? And if somebody doesn't show up here tomorrow night, no questions asked. Okay?"

"All right," she said. "But we still got to split the room rent."

She had a practical mind.

We hit the beach right after breakfast the next morning. It was only ten o'clock but already it was crowded, spotted with little knots of people on a patchwork of blankets. Nobody seemed to be alone. Most of the bodies were nicely bronzed, meaning they'd been out there since Memorial Day—a six-week head start on us. A few transistors were banging out the usual music and now and then there was an eruption of laughter, the ho-ho kind that you hear from ingroups.

"So," Denise said. "What do we do?"

We were standing there on a dune, surveying the scene like a couple of explorers, holding our blankets and our tote bags, peering through our wide-frame shades. The question was where to spread our blankets. You don't want to go too close to everybody else, since that seems obvious; but you don't want to go too far away either and give the wrong impression—that you're there purely for the sun.

"Maybe we ought to split up," Denise said.

"Why?"

"I can tell you why," she said. She was a trim little blond with the figure for a bikini but not the nerve, even in this day and age. She chewed gum in private but never in public; different people have different kinds of common sense.

"Tell me why," I said.

We were still standing there, holding our goddamned blankets and bags, and everybody had noticed us by now. Already, I knew, we had probably been pegged as a couple of weekend thrill-seekers from the Bronx looking for something to talk about during Monday's coffee break.

"Because," she said, "sooner or later some guy is going to sit down on my blanket and ask me all the usual crap about where I live and what I do, and this time I'm going to give him a line. Instead of working for the phone company I'm going to be a fashion model, and I've traveled to Europe and the Orient, and a whole line of crap, and I won't be able to do it if you're lying there grinning into your cleavage."

So we split up, agreeing to meet at dinnertime to swap yarns.

I walked down from the dunes, heading for a spot near the water. A few sun-scorched bodies rolled lazily on their blankets as I passed. My instinct was to smile at them and say, "Hi, guys. I'm Terry from the Bronx with only two days in which to do it all, so don't just lie there." But you're not allowed to do that. There are rules. You have to walk as if you're alone in the desert, be very cool to all the staring as if the staring is impolite and insulting; and all the while you feel yourself steaming up inside with pride in your body and with desire and anticipation, hoping it won't be *too* long before they start their checker game and make the jump to your blanket.

When I got to the spot I wanted I put down my tote bag, unfolded my blanket, swept it into the air like I was launching a magic carpet, and let it float down to the sand. Then, very casually, I undid the knee-length terrycloth beach robe I was wearing and sort of let it glide back from my shoulders to unveil myself. I dropped the robe onto the blanket, then raised my arms and pretended for a moment to fuss with my hair. When you look good in a bikini—and I do, goddamnit—you might as well show it. I stood there for maybe five or ten seconds with my fingers doing nothing at the back of my neck, one foot up on my toes, knee advanced.

Then I sat down, slowly, comfortably. You can do an awful lot, and project an awful lot, when you're at ease with your body. I lay down and adjusted my shades, and raised one knee, feeling warm and inviting in my snug little bikini. I closed my eyes; I preferred hearing their voices before seeing their faces. It was fun to try and determine what they looked like from the sound of their voices. I was usually wrong.

Well, it didn't take long. Maybe ten minutes, and considering the way I looked in the bikini (I may not be Ph.D. material but I do make up for it in other areas), that was about eight minutes longer than it should have been. I realized that something was blocking the sun; even with my eyes closed I could see that shadow there.

I kept my eyes closed and waited. My mind idled on what his opener might be. I wasn't twenty yet and I believed I'd heard every possible opening line (except "Hello"); but, of course, I'd never been to the Hamptons before. My feeling was that it was going to be different from Jones Beach.

Well, I waited. I swear he stood there for two minutes before saying anything, and if you don't think that's a long time under those circumstances, then think again. My curiosity began building until I started to wonder if maybe my bikini had somehow become unknotted or something and left him tongue-tied, or that maybe he was a fag being initiated into a fraternity and this was an unfamiliar and unthrilling experience for him. Still I wouldn't open my eyes. I could see his shadow shaped against the sun, a blur of head and shoulders. Then I began to wonder what *my* opener ought to be, in case the son of a bitch decided to stand there all day. If he didn't move soon I'd be going home with a head-shaped white patch in the middle of my sunburn.

"Excuse me."

At last. It wasn't the most brilliant opener I'd ever heard, but at least it was something.

I opened my eyes and lifted my shades.

"Yes?"

The excuse me, which had been spoken in a pretty good baritone, had suggested a sturdy male, and for once the eyes inside my ears weren't lying; they had, if anything, been underestimating. This guy was built like a halfback, with strong hairy legs, muscular arms that hung down from the sexiest sloping shoulders, and a chest that looked armor-plated. He had black hair down to the shoulders. His face was ruggedly handsome, with a very intense, humorless expression. The excuse me, now that I had a moment to consider it, had not been friendly at all—not unfriendly either, but sort of impersonal, as if he had misplaced the ocean and was going to ask directions.

"There's a party this evening at Fifty-one Jolly Street. At nine-thirty. Would you like to attend?"

"You're inviting me to a party?"

"Yes."

"I'll try to make it," I said.

"We look forward to seeing you," he said. Then he turned and walked away. I watched him. What a great back, I thought. There was this terrific tension in his whole body, like he had a pin sticking in him and was trying to ignore it.

He returned to a group of about eight people, mostly men, but with two real showcase broads lying there with breasts jutting up like howitzer shells. He kneeled down in front of this one guy who was sitting on a low-slung beach chair and spoke to him. The guy was wearing dark glasses and the cigar he was smoking was pointed straight out at the water like a rifle. He had curly blond hair, cut short, and looked kind of square. But he was the one the sexy one reported to. He nodded to the message and I waited for him to look over at me, but he didn't. He'd seen me, I guess.

"But who are they?" Denise asked.

"Guys giving a party, that's who," I said.

"You didn't get their names or anything?"

"Fifty-one Jolly Street, nine-thirty; that's their names. What's the difference what their names are? It's a party."

We were having dinner in a little Italian restaurant. I hadn't seen her all day, until I returned to the motel.

"Where were you today?" I asked.

"I met seven guys named Harold, all dentists," she said dismally.

"Which one did you pick?"

"The seventh one. His office is in Manhattan; all the others were from Queens. We walked on the beach and he bought me lunch. Then we went swimming and he got a cramp. We spent the rest of the afternoon on the beach."

"Why isn't he buying you dinner?" I asked.

"He said he had a date he couldn't break, that he'd meet me at nine o'clock."

"Bring him to the party."

"He's a dud."

"Then come with me."

"No, I'd rather stick with a known dud than meet new ones. I don't want to have to go through the whole thing again: where I live, where I work, my problems, his problems. He asked me to psychoanalyze him."

"Did you?"

"I told him I didn't have office hours on Saturday. Christ, I have to come all the way out here to meet these guys?"

"Then come to the party." I really didn't want to go alone.

"No. I may get a free periodontal treatment out of all this."

"You're going to have to do more than psychoanalyze him, sweetie," I said.

"Mind your business, sweetie," she said.

Chapter Three

I got to the party at ten o'clock, wanting to make a late entrance but not wanting to be *too* chic about it. The house at 51 Jolly Street was a cool-looking bungalow not far from the beach. It stood off by itself, with trees around it, and gave the impression that whoever owned it was a stickler for privacy.

I walked past it once, kind of to size it up and also because in my old age I was suddenly feeling shy. I wished Denise had come along. I could see people in the windows behind the trees, and there was calypso music but not too many decibels of it. It didn't seem like the wildest party ever, but maybe that was just as well. I wasn't in the mood for any lease-breaking hilarity, especially by myself. It was after a swinging pot party in the Village that I lost my virginity (what was left of it, anyway); not that I minded, but I would at least like to have been there when it happened. The guy didn't speak English, so I don't even know in which language it was that I got deflowered.

I walked the length of the street, out to the water, stared at it for a few minues, then turned and went back. I kept having peculiar misgivings about this party, but I knew that if I didn't go I'd have no story to tell for the weekend. Denise, at least, had Harold the Seventh, the good dentist; if I didn't do something tonight it was going to be a long ride home tomorrow.

So I went up onto the porch and rang the bell. It occurred to me that I didn't even know the name of the guy who had invited me. I supposed it didn't matter. I was wearing a miniskirt and a low-cut sweater (Denise said that when I bent over in that outfit, fore and aft I had no secrets) and I looked pretty good; I knew it and I felt it.

The door was opened by the guy who'd invited me. He

was wearing a white sport shirt unbuttoned to his navel and he was holding a drink in one big fist. He smiled just a little, showing deep crease marks in his cheeks. He didn't look so good close up.

"Well, I made it," I said, turning on my party personality.

"Come in," he said.

"You never did ask me my name," I said as he closed the door behind me.

"What is your name?"

"Terry."

He apparently didn't have a name, or else maybe he'd forgotten it. In any event, he brought me over to the bar and made me a gin and bitter lemon. I thanked him and started sipping until I realized I didn't like gin and hadn't asked for the drink.

There were about fifteen people in the room, with a fairly even division of the sexes. The men all seemed in their thirties, the women much younger. The women looked kind of used, if you know what I mean. None of them could have been past twenty-five, but the bloom was long gone from each of them. They all seemed cut from the same mold, with shiny hair and hoop earrings and little skirts or skintight pants and tight blouses or sweaters and spiked heels and toothy delight whenever one of the guys made a joke.

I didn't particularly care for the looks of any of the men; they appeared to be the type of guys who glance at you with the corners of their eyes and who smile slowly, like smiling was good manners and nothing more. They looked me over like I was the latest model car being unveiled. And the broads were sizing me up on the sly, trying to appear as if they weren't, with half-glances and heavy-lidded stares.

The guy who had invited me—he still didn't have a name—took me by the arm, gently but firmly, and led me across the living room out to the sun deck. Sitting there on a wicker chair was the one with the curly blond hair. He hadn't changed that much, was still smoking a cigar and wearing the dark glasses; the only difference was he had on a shirt and the ocean was gone.

"Mr. Monte," my guide and escort said to him, "this is Terry."

Mr. Monte smiled at me, his teeth clenched around the cigar, his eyes hiding behind the shades. He opened his hand and offered me a seat in the chair opposite him. When I sat down in the crunchy wicker chair the other guy disappeared. From where I was sitting I could watch the party. A few people were dancing now, one big blond shaking a pair of enormous bazooms to the calypso sounds; it was a good thing she was wearing a bra—otherwise she would have knocked herself cold.

"Are you enjoying yourself, Terry?" Mr. Monte asked.

"I don't know," I said. "I just got here."

"Do you like parties?"

"Sure."

"You look like the sort of girl who likes to enjoy herself."

"Everybody likes to enjoy themselves," I said.

"That's not true," he said. He had a low, smooth voice that sounded self-conscious about being low and smooth. "Some people are not happy unless they're miserable."

"Well," I said with a shrug, "as long as they're happy."

"Do you come often to the Hamptons?"

"First time."

"How do you like it?"

"It's pretty," I said.

It's hard to tell what somebody wearing dark glasses looks like, but I didn't think he was any beauty. I figured him for the sad side of forty, and he looked peculiar with that blond hair; I guess it didn't fit his personality. His nose appeared to have stopped a fast-moving fist at one time or another—it was slightly out of whack. But he was cool, just sitting there puffing on that cigar like it was the rarest delicacy this side of corned beef.

"How long are you planning to stay?" he asked.

"Till tomorrow."

"That's a pity. It's too bad you can't stay for the week. It's much nicer out here then."

"You stay here all week?" I asked.

"All summer," he said, lifting the cigar away from his mouth and shooting a stream of smoke into the soft summer night.

All summer! That sounded like the heart and soul of a dream—all summer at the beach, especially Mondays to Fridays; no New York sweltering, no blistering concrete, no blast-furnace subways, no sense of broiling air and soaking humidity glued to your skin—just basking in the sun, fanned by the ocean breezes, taking a dip whenever you felt like it, and at night the sound of the ocean and a black sky tossed with a billion stars.

"Boy, I envy that," I said.

"It's nice to be able to live that way," he said mildly.

"What do you do for a living?" I asked, zinging in the old party question. There was a set of them: What do you do? Whom do you do it for? Do you have a car? Do you dance?

"I'm in the importing business," he said.

"What do you import?"

"Things."

Okay, Terry, so he told you. Better not pursue it.

"And you?" he asked. "What do you do for a livelihood?"

"I'm a typist. With an insurance company. It's very exciting," I said with a false laugh, letting him know that I was hip.

"Where do you live?"

"In the Bronx."

Now, for some reason, he took off his dark glasses and looked at me, a most puzzled expression in his face.

"You live in the *Bronx*?" he asked.

"There are worse places," I said, feeling guilty as hell for some reason.

"And better," he said quietly, putting his glasses back on. "What is someone like you doing in the Bronx?"

"I'm living at home; it's the only place I know where the rent's paid."

He grunted.

"It's a pity," he said, "that someone like you should

have to worry about something that is as abundant in the world as money. What a shame."

"I'll go along with that," I said, laughing. I knocked down the rest of my drink, then slouched in my chair and crossed my legs. Even with his eyes lost behind those doomsday shades, I knew what they were looking at.

"Louis," he called out, and the one who had invited me came out to the deck (so he had a name after all). "Terry wants another drink," Mr. Monte said.

"Make it a screwdriver," I told Louis, handing him the glass and giving him a sweet smile. "With pineapple juice. And thank you."

He gave me a wise-assed smile, as if his running drinks for me was very funny. Then he went out.

Mr. Monte puffed serenely on his cigar and stared off into the distance.

"How unhappy are you with your life?" he asked.

"I never said I was unhappy."

He seemed to think about it for a minute, then he took off his glasses and gazed sternly at me, like he was making an in-depth evaluation. I matched him eye for eye.

"How would you like to spend the rest of the summer out here?" he asked.

"I can't afford it," I told him right back, kind of tough-voiced.

"It won't cost you a nickel."

"Are you propositioning me?"

Louis returned at that moment with the drink, handed it to me, and disappeared again. Mr. Monte's glasses were still off and his gaze was still fixed on me. I was beginning to feel like merchandise.

"Sometimes there's a good reason why a beautiful and sensual young woman lives in the Bronx with her parents," he said. And added, with a quirky smile, "Because they belong there."

"Look, I didn't come here to be insulted," I said, which was about all I could muster.

"If you think what I just said is insulting, then perhaps you feel you *do* belong in the Bronx."

I held my drink in both hands and took a sip, giving

him a moody stare. I didn't like him, didn't like what he was saying, but at the same time couldn't escape the nagging thought that there was *some* truth in what he was saying. I raised the glass again and this time took a gulp. I could feel the vodka hitting the gin.

"What about those babes in there?" I asked, indicating with a lift of my chin. "What fate have you saved them from—Brooklyn?"

"Don't flatter them," he said. "They've been invited for the weekend only."

"You're somethin', you know that, Mr. Monte? Boy, you're really somethin'. You invite a girl to a party, talk to her for a few minutes, and then *wham*! ... you're propositioning her not for the night or even the weekend, but for the whole goddamned summer. Boy, you deal . . . *wholesal*e!"

I finished the drink. I could taste the vodka more than the pineapple juice. That S.O.B. Louis knew how to mix them.

"Louis," Mr. Monte called.

An empty glass was called a Louis. I was starting to feel giddy. Wholesale. *Hole sale?* Better keep that kind of joke to yourself, baby. Wait till Denise hears about this one. While she was scratching around for maybe a date for next Saturday with her dentist, maybe a movie in the Bronx, or, if she was lucky, theater tickets, in hot old New York, I was being offered a whole summer. Orange juice this time, I told Louis; I don't like your pineapples. He grinned at me. He knew, he knew. That drink came back so fast it was like he'd been holding it behind his back with his other hand. Which maybe he was. I don't know.

The idea of the whole thing! Not having to ride that damned subway downtown in the morning, jammed in with a thousand perverts whose fingers kept fumbling against my ripe ungirdled little can, starting a day's work already perspiring and irritated, and having tuna-fish lunches in crowded coffee shops with waitresses writing my order on little pads of lined green paper, and drinking my coffee with my left hand so as to keep the previous customer's lipstick stain on the far rim, and sitting all day typing that dull crap about actuarial tables and what a hell it is to make a typo when you've got six carbons in, and that dumb broad at the next desk who always looks at Mr. Baumann in his glass-enclosed office and whispers, "One of these days I'm going to tell him to wipe his ass with his onionskin paper," and who thinks that's so devastating, and then the goddamned subway home again with the perverts, and climbing out into the massed motionless air of the Bronx and sitting home and watching TV and listening to my mother say thank God for air-conditioning.

They were expecting me to go wrong anyway. My father was waiting for it, my mother dreading it. There were four little sisters behind me, and just because once I didn't come home from a Saturday-night party in the Village (the one that cost me my cherry), they had me penciled in as a degenerate threatening to poison the little sisters. Go out with nice guys—that was the refrain. Who's nice? That young lawyer they fixed me up with? They ought to know he took me to a party in Chinatown and asked me to blow him in the closet. When you're stacked like I am, the world ain't nice. And I don't think I dress "provocative" or "shameless." Those are the styles the best people wear, and that's my body. I can't be held responsible for the flesh of the female and the chemistry of the male. Sex is an old custom, like war and murder. Nice guys? What about that baby-food salesman they fixed me up with? He was married with two kids and his wife didn't understand him. And what about the "college professor"? He turned out to be a postgraduate student whose big dream was to sail a schooner around the Virgin Islands for the rest of his life. And what about that accountant they thought was so nice? How could I tell them he couldn't get an erection unless he put on silk stockings and a bra? My poor parents; they never learned that nine-tenths of the world is a fake, and that you're only young for about five years. Far be it from me to try and educate them. Their ignorance may have been bliss for them, but for me it was a royal pain in the bottom.

"You drugged me, you lousy son of a bitch!" I yelled.

"Hardly," he said.

"Then what happened?" I demanded.

"Gin, vodka, and in the end Scotch," he said.

"Why'd you give it to me?"

"Because you asked."

We were in the bedroom. I was curled up on the bed, still dressed, thank God; Mr. Monte was standing in front of an open closet that looked full of silky colors, just hanging away his shirt. He was bare-chested, but still wearing his pants, thank God. I didn't hear a sound from the rest of the house.

"Where is everybody?" I asked. "What happened to the party?"

"Everybody has gone home."

"Louis too?" I asked, as if I gave a crap about him.

"Louis doesn't live here. I live here."

"Who else?"

"No one else."

"You married?" I asked.

He gave me an annoyed look, as if I'd farted.

"What time is it?" I asked.

"Three o'clock."

"I gotta get out of here," I said, swinging my legs off of the bed and getting up. "Where are my shoes?"

"You threw them into the garden."

I sat back down and folded my hands in my lap. I took a deep breath and sighed. I felt lousy, like some kind of mush was boiling in my stomach.

"Did I vomit?" I asked.

"No."

"How long have I been out?"

"Since midnight."

"Who carried me in here?"

"Louis."

"He's a handy son of a bitch, isn't he? What does he do anyway?"

"Louis works for me."

"Hey—what the hell do you think you're doing?"

He was opening his belt, that's what he was doing. He

didn't stop either, he just opened his pants and lowered them and stepped out of them, one pointing knee at a time, then turned around and hung them up in the closet. So there was Mr. Monte in his jockeys. Not a bad physique, but not the best either. He had muscular arms but was a bit flabby around the middle. He had a big can.

"I'm going to bed," he said.

"Not with me you're not."

"That's up to you, Terry. Everything is up to you."

He came over and sat down next to me, put his arms around me and kissed me. Then he took hold of my breasts and I closed my eyes; I'm sensitive as hell there. He kissed my mouth, my chin, then down along my throat. He eased me back down on the bed and I felt his fingers on my thigh, and then right up to the V for victory. I squirmed modestly and moaned happily.

"You don't even have to go back home," he said. "We'll go out tomorrow and get you a whole new wardrobe."

"Are the shops open on Sunday?" I asked.

"Yes."

He picked me up and gently swung me around and stretched me out on the bed. He was very strong. My head was on the pillow, my eyes were still closed.

He raised my sweater and I helped him slide it over my head. Then he sprawled on top of me, jamming his whacker right up against me. He began kissing my breasts and then I put my arms around him. He was goddamned solid and muscular through the back and shoulders. Then my skirt was gone and only my little bikini panties were left between me and blushing. His fingers were under the elastic band, toying with it. The big moment was on the way—that instant when suddenly you're completely naked, when you can just spread your arms and legs and feel absolutely beautiful and free; that was one of the most exciting things about sex as far as I was concerned.

He was suffocating me with kisses—not long or sensual kisses, but a rat-a-tat-tat of breathless little pecks all over my face and throat and breasts. I could feel that peculiar kinky blond hair of his rubbing against my cheek.

"It's going to be a hell of a summer, baby," he whispered.

I just went "Mmmmmm," thinking: Holy shit, all of a sudden, right out of nowhere—a whole summer at the Hamptons. It was true I couldn't remember saying yes, but I sure as hell wasn't going to say no. But then a certain thought strayed in.

"What am I going to tell my parents?" I said. What a stupid time to say that, I told myself. Jesus Christ almighty, when the hell was I going to grow up?

He didn't even answer; either he didn't give a damn about my parents or else he didn't think this was the moment to discuss the question, which it surely wasn't.

I felt him rolling the panties down, all the way along my thighs and legs, like a little wriggling, right down to my ankles and then off. When I opened my eyes he was straddling me with his knees, his thumbs inside the elastic of his jockeys, about to take them down.

"Aren't you going to turn out the light?" I asked.

He was really to a steam now; he had a wild, lustful glare in his eyes. He looked at the bedside lamp, which was the only light on in the room. All of a sudden he leaned over, swung his arm out, and knocked the lamp clear off the table. It crashed to the floor and the plug came yanking out of the socket, giving us instant darkness.

That's how Mr. Monte turned out the light.

Chapter Four

It was Denise who first mentioned the word mistress to me. By this time it was the end of November and I was comfortably ensconced (I like the sound of that) in my little one-bedroom pad in the East Sixties. Ned—Mr. Monte—brought me there after the summer and said this was where I'd be living from now on. It was furnished in High Lush, with lots of soft chairs, deep carpeting, a small bar, an oval bed, and drapes as thick and heavy as canvas over the windows. Ned said to always keep them closed, day and night. He was paying the rent, so they stayed closed.

He moved me in on September 20 and there I was. I wasn't allowed to have my name on the letter box—it was marked Mr. Fritz, whoever the hell that was supposed to be—so I never even got a letter. I had a color TV though, and a telephone, for local calls only. All the bills—rent, phone, electric—went to Ned. I never saw anything. There were times when I didn't even see Ned. Sometimes as much as a week would go by and he wouldn't show. He never explained his absences and I never asked questions, which I knew he preferred. He never stayed for more than two days at a time, but when he was there it was great. We'd eat out at high-class restaurants and go to a show or a nightclub, and wherever we went it was always in a hired limo. One night in October we had a midnight supper at a classy French restaurant on East Fifty-fifth and then just rode in the limo all night till sunrise, in and out of every street in Manhattan. It's great to see the city that way; it's like you're watching it without being seen.

I can't say it didn't get lonely when Ned wasn't around. There was nothing to do all day but watch TV and try to outguess the dummies on the game shows and then get involved with the soap operas. I had a hundred dollars a week allowance, most of which went for food and clothes, mostly clothes. Ned liked me to dress flashy and always be wearing something different. But I couldn't go out much because he wanted me to be there when he showed up, and I never knew when that would be. He seldom telephoned, but would just pop up. Once I'd been out all afternoon doing the Fifth Avenue shops and when I got back he was there. He was really ticked off; in fact I thought he was going to swat me—he had a lot of violence in him. He cross-examined me in a real short-tempered way about where I had been and what I'd been doing. It took me a half hour to convince him I'd been shopping and to calm him down.

Now and then I had thoughts, of course. It got lonely in that apartment at times. The night doorman was a good-looking kid and was always sizing me up and I was tempted. But I knew if Ned ever caught us there would be hell to pay. Maybe if I'd known for sure he was going to be away I would have bedded the kid, but a couple times Ned walked in at four in the morning; it was as if he was letting me know he was unpredictable and that therefore I had better be predictable.

The business with my parents got settled quick. When I called them from the Hamptons that first weekend and told them I had decided to spend the summer they hit the ceiling.

"You're with a man, aren't you?" my father asked, his voice all full of anxiety, like a scientist about to hear his lifelong theory confirmed.

"No," I said.

"Liar!" he yelled.

He went on and on, telling me that I'd given them nothing but tension and aggravation all my life. Tension and aggravation—those were the things. And now he said he was not surprised. Well, if there had been any chance of being talked into coming back—and at that moment there still was—it went right out the window. I called my mother the next day, when I knew my father wasn't home, and she was pure ice. She wanted to know if it was all right for my sisters to wear some of my clothes and use some of my handbags.

"Ma," I said, "I'm not dead yet, stop divvying me up."

"If you're living in sin," she said, "you're dead."

I felt sorry for them. They were hurt and didn't really know how to express it. So, frustrated with their inability to handle the situation, they simply let the lid fly off. I think that's what happened. They said things to me I knew they couldn't have meant. I cried a lot those first few days and I knew they were crying too. I called now and then, just to let them know it wasn't so bad, that a person could survive sin and be happy; but they remained stone cold to me. I called them on Labor Day to say I would be coming in soon to see them. They told me not to bother, that it was too late, that I was no longer welcome there. They had to "protect" my sisters, they said.

"From what?" I asked.

"From you," my father said.

"That's bullshit," I said.

"Is that so?" he asked in a very arch way, as if hearing me speak English for the first time. Then he really astounded me. "Bullshit to you," he said, and hung up.

Denise was the only one I kept in touch with, but even she proved to be a lost cause. When I told her that first weekend that I wouldn't be going back with her she didn't say much. I told her that what I was doing wasn't very revolutionary, simply shacking up with a guy for the summer. Hardly an unnatural or unusual thing.

"You barely know him," she said.

"He seems okay."

"Why can't I meet him?"

"He's touchy."

"Terry, you'd better come back with me tonight."

"I'm tempted," I told her, and I was. "But I just can't."

"You're selling your soul."

"Come off it," I said. "Wouldn't you do it, for the right guy?"

"For the right guy, maybe."

"Anyway, it's the same thing—me shacking up for what I'm getting and you putting out to get your teeth fixed."

She didn't like that and I didn't see her until after the summer—not until October in fact. Then I called her for lunch. We ate in a ritzy little restaurant across the street from my building, at a window table—from where I could watch the building, just in case Ned happened to show up.

When I filled her in on what had been happening since the end of the summer, her eyes popped.

"I thought you'd simply moved out of your parents' apartment, changed jobs, and taken a place on your own," she said.

"Uh-uh."

"You mean this guy has fixed up an apartment for you, and furnished it, and everything . . . ?"

"Yep."

"And pays the rent, and everything . . . ?"

"Everything," I said.

She gazed at me in utter astonishment. Then she leaned forward across the table and said the word I hadn't thought of.

"You mean you're his *mistress?*"

I thought about it for a few moments, sort of turning it over and around in my head. Then I nodded.

"I guess I am," I said.

"You're a kept woman," she whispered, struggling to keep her voice down.

"Denise," I whispered back, "it isn't so terrible."

"Aren't you ashamed?"

"No."

"Is this what you want to do with your life?"

"Denise . . ." I said, starting to get teed off.

"It's degrading," she said.

"Denise, if you don't shut up I'm going to ram your breaded veal cutlets down your throat."

"I'm trying to help you," she insisted.

"Listen, did my parents give your brain a wash?"

"No. Your parents have thoroughly and categorically disowned you. And I can't say as how I blame them. Terry, what are you doing with your life?"

She said this just loud enough to cause cocked eyebrows at the next two tables, where some silver-haired executive-suite types were sitting. Knives and spoons and forks stopped in mid-air while the men paused to stare at us and listen. This was a restaurant of very intimate and subdued atmosphere, where lunch began at nine dollars a kick and everything was à la carte. It wasn't the kind of place where you raised your voice. (I'd brought Denise there to impress her—why, I don't know.)

Well, hell, I thought, she'd started it and I wasn't going to lower my eyes and play the mortified maiden.

"You're not exactly a candidate for the nunnery yourself, you know," I said, just loud enough to keep lunch in suspension at the next table.

"At least I pay my own way," she said.

"Listen, what about that dentist?" I asked. She turned quick to see who was listening, and then turned back to me and shaped her lips into a Shhh. "The last I heard he was about to drill you through every opening you had, as long as . . ."

"You bitch!" she yelled, hurling her napkin at me and getting up. That stopped the silverware in the whole goddamned restaurant now. For a second the place became dead silent, everybody sitting as motionless as a photograph. The maître d' closed his eyes for a moment and sucked his breath up through his nose. He hadn't been too happy to see us in the first place, especially Denise with her chintzy coat and funny hat.

"Bitch!" Denise yelled again, her voice going high and thin. Then she went racing out, chewing a mouthful of breaded veal. From my window seat I saw her come flying out of those solemn leather-covered doors and run into the street; then she turned around and came racing back in again to get her crummy coat. She tore it from the hands of the cloakroom lady, poked her head around into the dining room, yelled "Bitch!" at me one more time and then went flying back out to the street. She saw me from the sidewalk, gave me the finger, and then disappeared, running off as she struggled to put on her coat.

When I turned around everybody in the restaurant was staring at me.

"There's so much anxiety these days," I said to the

gentlemen at the next table, and rooted myself to the spot while I finished my lunch, dessert and all.

I was so damned excited. It was the first time Ned was taking me anywhere where there were people—I mean people to talk to, to mingle with. He'd called me at four o'clock.

"I'm picking you up at eight," he said (that's what I heard when I picked up the phone—no hello or anything). "We're going to a party at a friend's house. I want you to dress nice, not too cheap or flashy. Got it?" Then he hung up.

He showed up at eight on the button, wearing a black overcoat and a dark suit. He usually was a pretty casual dresser, going for sport clothes. But not tonight.

"What's the occasion?" I asked.

"I told you," he said. "It's a party. The wedding anniversary of some close friends. Very important people."

I was impressed; he never talked like that about anybody. I always had the impression that he thought *he* was the most important person in the world.

He stared critically at me. I was wearing an off-the-shoulder navy blue dress that went to the knees. This dress didn't show too much, but it sort of let you know it was there.

"You wearing a girdle?" he asked.

"If you have to ask, then . . ."

"Put one on," he said. "These are very respectable people."

He followed me into the bedroom. I took off my dress and stood in my bra and panties. He was watching me; he liked to watch me dress and undress. Most men like watching a woman dress and undress; and a woman enjoys it when she knows a man is enjoying it. The trick is to pretend you're unaware of the staring while you're doing it; do everything nice and casual.

"And I don't want you to go talking to anybody tonight," he said, watching me hoist the girdle into place.

"Why not?" I asked reaching for my dress.

"Because I tell you. Just stick close to me."

It made me think of the girls who had been at the party that first night in the Hamptons, the ones who had stood around and laughed at everybody's jokes and never said a word on their own. I'd thought at the time they were just zombies, but maybe they'd been under orders too, told to keep their mouths shut and make the boys look bright and witty. But that wasn't my style; I was a natural jabber, especially after a couple of drinks.

Ned had hired a limo, a big sleek beauty a half-block long, with an engine so smooth it must've been made of talcum powder. If it wasn't for the changing scenery you would never have thought you were moving. There was a glass divider between us and the driver that went up and down like a guillotine, and it kept going up and down until Ned told me for Christ's sake to stop fooling with the buttons.

He didn't say much as we drove out to Long Island, where the party was; in fact, he seemed pretty uptight. He was sitting with his arms folded and his legs crossed.

"I've missed you, honey," I said, trying to brighten him up.

He didn't say anything.

"Why do you have to stay away so much?" It was true that I missed him, but only because he was the only person I ever saw.

"It's none of your business," he said.

"I'm just telling you I get lonely, that's all."

"You're *supposed* to be lonely when I'm not there."

That was about the limit of any sympathy I'd get from him, I knew. But anytime I felt myself starting to get ticked off I'd remember that I used to take a lot of crap on the job, too, sitting at a typewriter all day for a big fat $120 a week, and then at the end of the day having to pay for the privilege of riding in the subway. The man sitting next to me had taken me away from all that. If he wanted to be a bastard now and then he was entitled.

"Whose party is it anyway?" I asked, trying to make conversation.

"I told you, close friends. It's their twenty-fifth wedding anniversary."

"Twenty-five years," I said, shaking my head. "Christ, can you imagine?"

"No," he said.

"They were married before I was born."

"What's so remarkable?" he said crankily. "Weren't your parents?"

"*My* parents?" I laughed. "You bet your kiester."

"Listen," he said, turning to look at me, "you watch your goddamned language once we get there. These are very respectable people."

"I'll be a perfect lady," I said.

The house had to be seen to be believed. It was on the South Shore, right on the water. You drove down an incline to reach it and it just seemed to be coming up at you, big and white and shiny. A long circular drive around a spread of green lawn lit up by spotlights brought you to the front door. The porch had enormous white pillars, like a Southern mansion. Behind the house I caught a glimpse of a boat house and a private dock and the water. Off to the side was the parking lot and it was filled with other limos and some Cadillacs and one tank that looked like a Rolls.

A guy dressed like an ensign, cap and all, escorted us inside. There must've been a hundred people there, mostly an older crowd. Waiters with trays of drinks were circulating and I started off with a martini. A five-man combo was playing dance music out of the 1940s. This wasn't a swinging affair, but it was elegant. The room everybody was gathered in had marble floors and great big cut-glass chandeliers, and it all looked like something out of a Louis the Fourteenth movie.

Then this big chesty guy was coming toward us. He looked to be about fifty, but he had a youthful spring and zest about him that was positively sexy. He had silver hair, tanned face, and a most winning smile. I noticed that everybody stared at him when he passed and I figured him to be an especially big gun here. He was holding a long cigar in his hand and he stuck it between his teeth and reached out to greet Ned.

"Glad to see you, Neddie," he said in a growl like a friendly St. Bernard.

"Good evening, Mr. Corbett," Ned said, ever so polite. "Congratulations."

Mr. Corbett's eyes then set upon me with what I can only describe as a fondling glance.

"Good evening, young lady," he said quietly.

"This is Terry, Mr. Corbett," Ned said. "Terry, say hello to our host."

"Hello, our host," I said.

"It's very good to see you," Mr. Corbett said, taking my little dainty hand in his big brawny one and squeezing it for a moment.

"I love your house," I said.

"Do you? I'll have to show you around later."

"I'll look forward to it."

He smiled again, studying me, the big cigar angling out. Then he went away, striding briskly, his approach forcing little openings for him through the crowd.

"What the hell's the idea being so pushy?" Ned whispered angrily, moving me along by the elbow.

"I was just trying to be gracious, that's all."

"I told you to keep your mouth shut."

So that's what I did for the next couple of hours—kept my mouth shut. I think it was that night that my little blue eyes began to open and I had my first inkling that there was something definitely shady about Ned. It wasn't anything he said or did, but the way his friends were. What it was—they all seemed to be so self-conscious and uptight, afraid of being open and natural. They were polite, reserved, and for a big party in honor of a happy occasion, there was very little drinking—in fact nobody got smashed.

Ned kept me at his side most of the time, so I heard a lot of his conversations with his friends. I can only describe them as conversations in which, deliberately, nothing was said. Maybe it was because I was there, and they were wary of talking business in front of a stranger (that's what men talk about most—business—with the same intensity and detail with which they discussed sex when they were boys). Now and then there was a joke for me to laugh at, and they were pretty small potatoes—warmed-over stuff you heard on TV ten years ago.

After about two hours there was a buffet dinner, and then after that some of the men—Ned among them—followed Mr. Corbett upstairs and were gone for almost an hour. (It was something to see them going up the stairs; about fifteen guys like Ned, guys who looked like they were in command wherever they went and never took crap from anybody, trooping up those stairs behind Mr. Corbett like so many pups to be fed, and him walking like a field marshal, as if he was used to having a troop at his back.)

Without my keeper, and not knowing anybody, I felt out of place. I was surprised that none of the men came over, if not to flirt, then at least to say hello. That was almost expected wherever you went, but it didn't happen here. I wandered out to one of the terraces overlooking the water. It was absolutely lovely. From where I stood I could see Mr. Corbett's private dock; there was a cabin cruiser tied up there. *What a way to live!* I wondered where he got his money, but then struck the thought right out of my head, as if Ned would somehow know about it.

I thought I was alone on the terrace, but then I became aware of someone else. It was a woman, sitting in a chair in the corner, next to some potted plants that grew higher than the railing. She smiled when I looked at her, as if she'd known I was going to notice her sooner or later.

"Hi," I said.

"Are you enjoying yourself?" she asked.

"Who wouldn't?" She didn't say anything, but kept smiling, though now the smile was kind of sad. "Aren't you?" I asked.

She got up and walked toward me. She was a tall, beautifully built woman, probably in her middle forties. Her reddish hair was swept up and she was wearing a gorgeous floor-length gown that must have put a considerable dent in somebody's checkbook. She looked like an immensely proud woman, and intelligent, too; but there was this sadness in her face as if her intelligence was nagging her with the information that she hadn't lucked out too well in certain things in spite of appearances.

"What is your name?" she asked.

"Terry."

"You came with Ned Monte, didn't you?"

"That's right."

"Is he your beau?"

"Well, I don't know how you'd call it."

"How would *you* call it?"

I shrugged, not knowing how to answer. She reached out and took my hand and held it firmly for a moment.

"I'm sorry," she said. "I'm not trying to embarrass you. I have no right to."

She walked to the corner of the terrace and stared out at the water. I followed her and leaned over the terrace, resting my boobs on the railing.

"That's a sweet-looking boat down there," I said.

"Do you like it? It's very expensive."

"I know."

"You don't know *how* expensive. Like the house. Like my jewelry. Like my gown."

"Everything's got a price tag." Worldly Terry talking.

"And everything is for sale, isn't it?"

"I guess so."

"Then everything is reduced to a commodity, isn't it? Even people. Don't you think that's too bad?"

"I don't know," I said, staring at that boat, thinking how nicely I could decorate the sun deck in my bikini on a hot sunny day. "I guess that's the way things are. Everybody's always talking about making a deal, getting their share, buying, selling, investing. That's what keeps the wheels turning."

"Are you happy, Terry?"

"Me? Personally? I guess so. Aren't you?"

She laughed, a little sound way back in her throat. "I never ask myself that question."

"I'm sorry," I said. "I didn't mean to pry. As a matter of fact, I had specific orders to keep my mouth shut."

She laughed again, in a knowing, sarcastic way.

"Did you ask why?" she asked.

"No."

"That's too bad."

"You're Mrs. Corbett, aren't you?"

She passed me a real shrewd look.

"And it's your anniversary," I said. "And you're unhappy."

"Does it show?"

"It sticks out like that diamond ring you're wearing."

Suddenly she put her hand on my cheek and leaned over and kissed me lightly on the mouth.

"You're very sweet, Terry," she said, "and understanding. Will you come out to visit sometime?"

"I'll have to ask Ned," I said, feeling a strange mix of things. I wanted to step back, away from her; but at the same time I felt sorry for her, and that was a damned peculiar thing, since here was a woman that had everything, twice over. Feeling sorry for someone like that is really a deep feeling.

At that moment a man appeared in the doorway. He was a short, fat man, and he looked uncomfortable.

"Hello, Al," Mrs. Corbett said.

He stood there for a moment, chewing on his lower lip, looking from Mrs. Corbett to me, back and forth.

"Mr. Corbett would like to see the young lady in his study," he finally said, and then you could hear him breathe out like a sigh, as though he was good and relieved to be rid of his message.

I didn't know what to do. I was really embarrassed. Mrs. Corbett gave me a twisted little smile, but her eyes were steady and cool.

"Perhaps he wants to give you a ride on the boat," she said.

I still didn't know what to do. She wasn't going to help any. I could see that. She was watching me, very expectant and curious.

"I guess I should go and see what he wants," I said, an apology in my voice.

"By all means," she said, her voice dead and dry.

As I walked past her, she said, "We can still be friends, Terry, can't we?"

I nodded.

Chapter Five

When I look back on it, I think I had a peculiar feeling as I approached that door. Looking back, the memory seems like a dream, and I see myself walking through all the other guests and they're absolutely silent, watching me, and that door is getting closer and bigger and more ominous looking. It was like I was walking down a tunnel that was getting narrower and narrower, and at the end of it was that door.

Al, the little fat man, walked me up to the door and said, "Go ahead in."

I looked at him for a moment, then reached out, took the doorknob, turned it, and went in. Entering the room, I closed the door behind me. It was a beautiful room, large and high-ceilinged, with heavy drapes covering the windows. There was a parquet floor with a great-looking Persian rug in the middle of it, and in the middle of that was Mr. Corbett's desk. Behind that was Mr. Corbett, smiling at me, a baton-sized cigar smoking between his fingers. The smile on his face was like saying: "We're very good friends, but you don't know it yet." I looked back at him with a kind of smirk, as if to tell him, "I know just what's going on in your head, Big Boy."

Then I spotted Ned. He was sitting in a chair in the corner, looking very glum. He gave me a moody stare, then turned away.

"Have a seat, Terry," Mr. Corbett said, pointing to a high-backed chair with a soft, swelling rump of a seat. I sat down on the edge of it, primly, knees and ankles together. From out of the corner of my eye I could see Ned; he was sitting there like a real sad sack, looking down into his lap.

"I've been having a conversation with Ned," Mr. Corbett said. "He's an old friend, a very good and highly valued old friend. After some discussion we've come to an agreement."

I just sat there and listened, trying to be as cool and detached as I could. I was a bit scared—obviously it was me they'd been discussing and agreeing about.

"Ned has graciously agreed to surrender his rights," he said. Now he put that cigar in his mouth and puffed a big cloud of smoke and leaned back behind it like some kind of genie or something and smiled at me, watching me with sharp, wryly amused interest.

"I don't think I understand," I said. "His rights?"

"To you."

"His rights to me?"

"Yes."

I gave Ned a quizzical look, but he was still studying his lap.

"Okay?" Mr. Corbett asked.

I understood completely, but I was still too dumbfounded to say anything, too dumbfounded to give it any straight thinking.

"Ned is a fine person," Mr. Corbett said. "A real friend. I'm proud of him and I'm grateful to him."

It began going through my head now like a windmill in a hurricane. Rights to me? What rights? To pay my rent, buy my clothes, and bed me down whenever he felt like it? Was that something you just signed over to somebody else like a goddamned car? But all I could think to say was, "What does he get in return?"

Mr. Corbett laughed—that great chesty laugh—like he had a sick dog growling inside him.

"We haven't discussed that yet," he said. "But I can tell you what it is—my gratitude, my lasting friendship."

I looked at Ned again; he didn't look too thrilled with his end of the deal.

"So it's done," Mr. Corbett said.

"Just like that?" I asked, looking back to him.

He spread his hands and shrugged.

"What else is there to say?" he asked.

I knew of a few things to say, but they were still too

scrambled in my head to have made any sense. Ned sure as hell wasn't saying much; he looked like a man who'd been outflanked and surrounded, who'd surrendered without too much of a struggle. Shafted, in a word. Then all of a sudden something struck me: Ned was in love with me. It hit me just like that and I believed it, not that I was trying to flatter myself, because frankly I found the whole idea sad and scary. I thought how stupid I'd been not to have realized it before, how Ned felt about me. It was simply that I'd been taught that love was something else, something tender and gentle. But now I realized there was all kinds of love, as many as there were people to give it. His way had been completely unknown to me, cold and stern and tough. But he had brought me out to this party—this very special thing, for him—because he was proud of me, because he wanted to show me off, because he was, in his way, in love with me. He was a man who could only feel, not give. Christ, I thought, the poor guy; he was in love and I'd never even known it. Maybe if I'd known I could have brought it out of him, helped him— not that I was in love with him, but simply because I believed love was too precious ever to be wasted or ill-used.

Then Mr. Corbett was saying, "All right, Terry. I'll see you later."

I left with Ned. He had a firm grip on my arm as he hurried me through all the guests in the big room. I remember passing Mrs. Corbett and her fixing her eyes on me, shrewd and cool and sympathetic all at once, and I had the feeling she knew everything that had been said behind that door.

Ned ushered me out the front door into the night.

"All right," he said. "Wait here."

"For what?" I asked.

"The car."

"We're leaving?"

"You are."

He was grim, and tense as hell, looking off into the night for the car. I felt sorry for him. He hadn't been such a bad guy (already, without realizing it, I was thinking of him in the past tense). All of a sudden I felt I understood him. He just wasn't the sort able to let himself go and show his feelings, as though he believed such displays indicated weakness. Christ, if only men knew that the ability to show love, and to sometimes be gentle, makes them seem as strong as iron in the eyes of a woman; it makes them seem *real*, and that's where the true strength lies—in being real, in being human. But poor Ned, somebody had taught him all the wrong things, and he had learned them oh so well.

I guess I wasn't so sorry for Ned as I was for the thing that was happening to him, for the fact that it *could* happen and *was* happening; that was the awful thing—that people could get so mixed up with each other and inside of themselves that they could never take hold of the real things, the good and beautiful things. To feel it happening so close to you, to be part of it—that was the saddening thing.

"Ned..." I said.

"The car is coming," he said, still peering off into the night. He couldn't bring himself even to look at me. He was being all churned up inside, I could tell.

When the car came the guy who was dressed like an ensign went down the steps and opened the door for me. When I got in and the ensign had closed the door and backed away I looked up, but Ned was gone.

Slowly the big limo pulled away. I looked back, watching that big house and all its lights. It was like a glittering island in its own private ocean. It all seemed so wonderful and desirable.

Chapter Six

It was a long, quiet ride home, and some of my thoughts began to straighten out. There was the excitement, of course, thinking about the fact that the master of that house was interested in me. That was purely an ego thing. For a while I felt like some dumb little clerk who had just been given a big promotion, as though I was going to be moved from my little East Side pad and installed in that house, with all the servants and cars and the boat, too, at my disposal. I also had a fleeting thought about good friend Denise, about her going down for a goddamned dentist just to get a free ride in his chair. If you were going to compromise, I thought with a sudden unbecoming smugness, you might as well do it on the grand scale.

Then I began feeling a little bit scared. I don't know why precisely. Maybe it was because I still knew so little about these guys, because I was deliberately avoiding trying to think about who they were and where their money came from. I tried to tell myself it was none of my business, and that, anyway, if they were doing something illegal it had nothing to do with me. I was just a girl friend, somebody they looked in on when they felt like. Hell, my straitlaced, holier-than-thou father laid his bets with the local bookie, didn't he? What was so legal about that? For all I knew Mr. Corbett was the chief bookie of the Bronx and my father's dollars had helped build that house and pay for Mrs. Corbett's jewelry and perfume, which meant that my father's dollars were helping to pay for my life of sin. Boy, that was a cute way of looking at it.

After that I started to get sore. It began to occur to me that nobody had asked me my opinion about any of it.

Ned and Mr. Corbett had gone into a room and closed the door and decided to swap me around, just like that, without asking me what *I* might think about it. I knew that you gave up a hell of a lot when you allowed somebody to buy you your clothes and pay your rent, but I didn't think it reduced you to a piece of merchandise. What was it that Mrs. Corbett had said?—everything was reduced to a commodity, even people. Well, I didn't want to be a commodity. Christ, there was a pawn ticket out on me, body and soul.

My indignation kept getting hotter and hotter, and I finally decided I'd rather move back to the Bronx and listen to my parents' endless horseshit than allow people to keep redeeming that pawn ticket anytime they felt like.

When the limo pulled up in front of my building and the driver came around to open the door for me, I pushed it open myself and got out.

"Thanks, but no thanks," I said to him, hurrying past the confused guy into the building.

Upstairs, I continued to stay mad. I threw open the drapes that Ned had always insisted remain closed and stood at the window and looked out at the city. The view was north, toward the Bronx, and it was like I was being told something. I could stay here and be a commodity or I could go back up there. There didn't seem to be any in between that was acceptable. Not even this apartment—I couldn't afford the place on my own; the goddamned rent was a goddamned $525 a month. And once you've been wearing nice clothes ... well ... you get used to wearing nice clothes; and you get used to supper clubs and good restaurants and travel, and you get used to *not* riding the freaking subway and having your freaking ass squeezed by freaking freaks.

I felt like calling some of my old friends, to see how life was treating them. It had been only a few months since I'd last seen them, since I'd last set foot in their world, but, Christ, it seemed like years. There was no point in calling them. Nothing would have changed with any of them; I was the one who was changing, who had changed, and so there was nothing I could say to them or them to me. All of those old solid virtues which had once made us friends and kept us together were now the very things that stood in the way.

I was too damned mad to go to sleep, too damned mad to watch television, too damned mad to do anything except stride around that apartment in my high heels and my knee-length "respectable" dress, which apparently hadn't been respectable enough. I stopped to pull down the damned girdle and threw it aside, then kicked off the high heels.

And then at about two o'clock I heard a key in the door. I was sitting in a chair with my arms folded and my legs crossed, and I jumped right up, figuring it was Ned. All of a sudden I was really looking forward to seeing him and was all excited.

But it wasn't Ned.

It was Mr. Corbett.

He closed the door behind him and walked into the place, looking around with a critical eye, like a man with the soul of an interior decorator.

"A picture ought to be on that wall," he said, pointing to a bare spot over the sofa. "And this carpeting is going to have to be picked up and replaced. It's not good enough."

I looked down at the carpeting; it had always seemed good enough to me.

He walked past me into the bedroom. And then he roared.

"An oval bed! Whose idea was that? What kind of crap is that? That's got to go. And you've got too many chairs in the bedroom. Get rid of one. What the hell do you need chairs in the bedroom for? And whose idea was it to paint one wall red? It looks like a New Orleans cat house."

He came out of the bedroom. I was standing in the middle of the living room, arms folded, giving him my iciest look. He seemed kind of weary. His tie knot was lowered and his top shirt button open. He took off his jacket and dropped it on the couch. Then something else caught his eye.

"That lamp stinks," he said.

"I happen to like it," I said.

Now he looked at me, a mixture of amusement and impatience in his eyes.

"It's got to go," he said.

"Ned bought it," I said.

"Ned doesn't live here anymore."

"He paid for everything."

"And I pay Ned," he said flatly. "And I say that lamp has got to go."

"Okay," I said. "Okay, Mr. Boss, Mr. Emperor."

And with that I bent down, unplugged the lamp, picked it up from the table, carried it over to the window, opened the window, and threw the lamp out into the night. I waited a few seconds and then heard it hit the street—twelve floors below. It made a soft breaking sound, like a light bulb hitting. Then I realized I could have killed somebody, and discreetly I peered out. The shattered lamp was lying in the middle of the street, its big white shade some twenty feet away. A couple of people were walking toward it, one of them looking up.

Mr. Corbett laughed.

"Kill anybody?" he asked.

"What else don't you like?" I asked coming away from the window. "The carpeting? The chair?"

He sat down on the sofa, laughing, shaking his head.

"Ned said you were a pisser," he said.

"I want you to get out," I said.

"Why should I? This is my apartment now."

"Okay," I said. "Then I'll get out."

I started to head for the door but he was up on his feet in a flash, taking hold of my wrist.

"Where do you think you're going?" he said. He was firm more than menacing or unfriendly.

"I'm trespassing in your apartment. I'm getting out."

"You're also wearing my clothes."

"Ned paid for them."

"And I pay Ned," he said.

"He works for his money, doesn't he?"

"Sure he does; but he's overpaid. So I figure when he's pissing away money, it's *my* money."

"All right, I'll mail the clothes back to you."

"I don't trust the U.S. mails."

Then I did a dumb thing—I was getting so goddamned furious. I took off my dress and threw it on the floor. Which left me standing there in my bra and snappy little panties.

"There's your goddamned dress," I said. "It will look good on you."

"Okay," he said. "Now you can go."

Very funny. Now I really felt like a damned fool, standing there like that. How can you make a serious moral argument when you're standing in your underwear and the other person is dressed? Nevertheless, I tried.

"You've got your nerve," I said, "you and your goddamned friend. What makes you think you can just trade me around like that? I'm a human being, not a commodity. The slave days are gone, in case you haven't heard. Did you ever take *me* into consideration when you were making your deal? Don't you think it makes some difference to *me*?"

"Does it?" he asked coolly.

"Of course it does."

"Bullshit," he said, making a sour face. "He could have been a three-legged monkey—but as long as he was paying the rent and buying you all those fancy outfits, he would've been beautiful. Look, kid, you've made a choice, you've chosen a lifestyle for yourself, and you like it; I know damn well you like it. You can pitch it away if you want—that's up to you. But you'll be sorry. Look, Ned is no beauty. Why'd you go with him? Why'd you agree to this in the first place?"

"It's the principle of the thing," I said. "You're trading me around. Don't you think I have any pride?"

"If you have any pride," he said with some heat in his voice now, "it ought to be swelling up just about now."

"Why? Who the hell are you? You're a fat, fifty-year-old guy who happens to have a lot of money."

Now he got sore. He took hold of my arm and squeezed it so I knew I'd have finger marks in it for a week.

"It's not fat, it's muscle," he said, scowling. "And I'm

not fifty, I'm forty-seven. And you bet your little pink asshole I've got a lot of money. I could have any broad between here and Hong Kong—but I want you."

He scared me a little. I twisted my arm free of him and backed away.

"What about your wife?" I yelled. I was starting to cry; it was dumb, but I couldn't help it.

"What about her?" he demanded. He didn't like this, I could tell.

"Don't you care about her?"

"What the hell has that got to do with you?"

"She's miserable," I said. "She told me so herself."

"You spoke to Helene? When?"

"Tonight."

"What did she tell you?"

"She's miserable, that's what. Your own wife. And I don't blame her—here you are, on your wedding anniversary, screwing off with me. If you can do that to her, what the hell happens to *me*? I'm just a piece of tail that caught your eye, for a month maybe, or a week, or maybe just for one night."

Now he pointed his finger at me and jabbed it a few times before he talked.

"You keep the hell away from my wife," he said.

"I felt sorry for her."

"I'm telling you, Terry." He was very serious; the mean side of him was in his eye.

"She invited me to come visit," I said, rubbing the tears from my eyes. "She's lonely."

"She's a sick woman," he said after a pause.

"She liked me."

"I'll bet," he said under his breath, like to himself.

"So how can I be with you?"

"You can be with me. It has nothing to do with anybody but us."

Now all of a sudden he put his arms around me and held me against him. He didn't kiss me, just held me. I got the peculiar feeling that he really wanted to do this, that he had the need to do it—just to hold me against him. After a few moments I put my arms up and around him. He was right: that wasn't fat, it was all muscle. He squeezed me harder against him.

""You're all right, Terry," he said. "You're a good person. I'm sorry if you were offended by what happened. I didn't like doing it, but I couldn't think of any other way. What the hell was I going to do, start courting you like a teenager? When you're used to getting what you want, you sometimes..."

He didn't seem able to finish. So I did it for him.

"Are crude."

He looked down at me and we began to laugh. He had a great smile, it really warmed up his face. I was laughing through my tears, and what a strangely terrific feeling that is—like a great shaking relief.

"Now," he said, letting go of me. "Put your dress back on. When I make love... I like to start at the beginning."

Chapter Seven

That was Charley. Tough and unpredictable. All man. Sometimes gentle, sometimes tender, and sometimes very moody. And generous to a fault, as the saying goes—except that I could never see any fault to generosity. He really poured it on—clothes, jewlery, all kinds of gifts. He even moved me into the Waldorf for a week while he had the apartment done over the way he liked it, and it really was much better. He had great taste. When we went out to dinner he knew which wines to order, knew the names and the years and all that kind of thing. Now and then he even brought me a book to read—something by Ernest Hemingway or Charles Dickens—and said I ought to read it because I might enjoy it. (The Hemingways I liked, but the Dickenses I found old-fashioned.) And unlike Ned, Charley was there a lot—three or four nights a week—and often stayed a whole weekend.

And the travel. Especially that first year. That winter we went to Nassau for a week and stayed on Paradise Island. Charley was terrific at the crap tables. One night it seemed like everybody in the casino was crowded around watching him throw the dice. He kept hitting his point and piling up his bets, pulling back when he thought the dice were getting old, and then piling it on again. He won thousands and thousands—and all the while he was shooting he kept one arm around me. We also went to Miami a couple of times, once just for a weekend. And then there were trips to Vegas. We toured all of the hotels and clubs, staying up till dawn and sleeping till three o'clock in the afternoon. Charley knew everybody, it seemed. Through him I met all kinds of big shots from the political world, like congressmen and judges, and a lot of big-time show-biz people.

With Charley you never knew what was going to happen next, and that's what was so exciting. I'll never forget those phone calls—"Be ready in an hour, we're going to Acapulco." That was typical. Once we taxied over to the 79th Street Boat Basin, and there was his boat tied up, waiting for us. With a hired captain at the wheel, we cruised up the Hudson to Bear Mountain. Charley sent the captain off to a motel for the night and we slept on board. It was romantic as hell, sleeping on the water in a bedroom that had wall-to-wall carpeting.

And sometimes he would want to do the simplest damned things. One Sunday morning we packed a picnic lunch and drove out to a park on Long Island and pitched our blanket on the grass and sat there and ate our sandwiches. But that it was all wrong and not built to last I realized that day at the simple picnic. Two young couples were sitting at a picnic table nearby and after a while they got to looking at us and whispering among themselves. I knew just what they were thinking. Charley wasn't noticing them, but it began to bother me. Finally I couldn't take it any longer and yelled over to them, "He's my father!"

They began to laugh and Charley looked around.

"They bothering you?" he asked me, frowning.

Before I could answer—and I was going to say no, sorry now that I had opened my mouth—one of the guys said to the other, loud enough for us to hear, "Sure he's her Daddy—like in Sugar."

There was no sense trying to stop Charley. He was up on his feet and striding across the grass toward those people. I didn't say a word. I didn't want to be one of those hysterical females who sit and scream, especially when I know it's not going to do any good.

The guys weren't too smart. Instead of getting up and apologizing while there was still time, they got up and smirked. They were tall kids, but tall like basketball players, lanky. Not hearing any apology, Charley waded in and, I swear, with two punches, first a left and then a right, he flattened those kids. One was knocked back across the picnic table and I can still see a paper cup full of beer bouncing up with the beer spurting into mid-air like a little arc of spittle; the other was flattened on the grass, falling so fast his legs never bent.

That was the last picnic we ever went on.

Through it all I never asked questions, and I knew Charley appreciated it. I knew that he and Helene weren't happy together, that he had a married son living in Chicago whom he seldom saw (and whom he never talked about), and that was about it. I knew Charley was in the rackets somehow, but I didn't know what and I seldom thought about it. Sometimes when we went to a club we'd sit with some pretty hard characters, especially in Miami. He even said some of the trips were business; I guess he knew he could tell me that because he knew I'd never ask him what business. He was completely relaxed with me—I could feel it—and it made me feel good.

So I didn't know what he was doing. No question it was something shady, but when I did give it a thought I figured it was bookmaking or numbers or something like that. (That's what I wanted it to be anyway, because I got a kick out of thinking that my father was betting with one of Charley's men.) Maybe I should have known better, and maybe there were times when I did suspect something else. But after a while you develop certain talents: you don't recognize what you see, you jumble what you hear, you forget what you know. It's easy, and it gets easier if all you do is center on yourself and think about having a good time, if you don't worry about who or what is paying for it.

I never thought about where it was all going with Charley and me. I guess it's true: When today is so much fun tomorrow doesn't count. You get corrupted by the good things, the good times, and that makes you short-sighted and selfish, and it makes the ice thinner and thinner. But I'm not going to preach, since everybody seems bent on finding out for themselves.

I guess you might say that in a way I was in love with Charley. He was nearly thirty years older than I—older than my father—but it didn't seem to make any difference. Some people might say it was sick, and there are others who would give out all kinds of complicated psychological theories—that I was using Charley as a father substitute and that sort of refined bullshit. But the truth was, very simply, I was in love with him. He was good to me—and was kind and generous and he never made me feel cheap.

And there was something else about Charley: he trusted me. He really did. I didn't realize how important that was to me until it happened. To be nineteen or twenty years old and to be trusted by somebody like Charley makes you feel mature all of a sudden. Every so often he would leave a valise behind in the apartment when he left, telling me not to touch it, that somebody would be by in a day or two to pick it up. And I never did touch it. I didn't even look at it. I didn't even *think* about it.

He was having a Fourth of July party at his house on Long Island and wanted me to be there.

"I can't Charley," I said. "I would feel funny."

"Why? Because of Helene? Don't worry about that."

"But she's your wife, and I'm . . ."

"You're going to be somebody else's date. You'll come in with somebody else. I won't even know who you are. But I want you there."

"But she knows what's going on."

He scowled, chewing the end of an unlit cigar. We were sitting in the living room. It was a warm summer's night and the window was open and you could see the uptown lights.

"How does she know?" he asked.

"Because she's no dummy."

He gazed at me, a sharp, almost hostile look in his eyes. I knew what was bothering him—Charley never liked to be contradicted or argued with in any way whatsoever.

"I want you there," he said. "I don't give a damn about her. It's my house. What the hell kind of party will it be if you're not there?"

There was no point arguing; he'd made up his mind.

"Whatever you say, Charley," I said.

"It'll be all right—don't worry. We'll all have a lot of fun."

I know somebody who didn't.

Charley sent an "employee" around to pick me up on Fourth of July morning. He was a quiet, dark-haired guy named Frankie. We drove out to the Island in his car and he didn't say two words during the whole trip. It was like he was transporting special merchandise or something. I tried to make conversation a few times—what the hell, it was a long ride—but he wouldn't pick up on anything. After a while I got the feeling he not only worked for Charley but was also scared shit of him.

There must have been about fifty or sixty people there. The party was behind the house, where the grass sloped down to the water. There were tables set up with white cloths; one was the bar, with two bartenders in charge, and the other tables were stacked with food, with everything from cocktail franks to fresh shrimp to fried chicken and cold cuts.

When I showed up with my silent shepherd Charley greeted me politely, saying it was nice seeing me again and even having the balls to ask how Ned was. It was a nice job of acting, but it didn't fool Helene one bit; I could tell that from the smile she gave me and the look in her eye—it was like one conspirator acknowledging another. But Helene was very friendly, and I admired her and felt sorry for her at the same time. She had a lot of poise, but I guess she *had* to have it; she had no choice. Privately, I thought Charley was being a real bastard for having me there.

Charley went around laughing and slapping everybody on the back and making a point of ignoring me, while Helene twice brought me plates of food and kept bringing me into her conversations with the other women.

"I'm disappointed that you've never visited," she said to me at one point.

"I'm sorry," I said. "I've been meaning to ... but I've been busy."

"I can imagine," she said quietly.

"You know how it is in New York," I said, forcing a laugh. "It never stops."

She smiled. I swear, she was the soul of understanding. I felt myself really envying her, and not just because she was married to Charley and had all that money and ease and no worries about her future; it was because she seemed so poised, so self-assured and secure, so absolutely comfortable with life. It's rare when you meet someone who doesn't seem to have any pettiness or hysteria in them. Here I was, screwing around with her husband, and there she was, being so goddamned polite and civilized to me. I'd heard about sophistication, but I guess I'd never really seen it until then.

I wondered if she screwed around. Somehow I doubted it, even though she had every good reason to; and that if she did, then it was because she really loved somebody and not out of spite to get even with Charley. She had too much class to just sack out with the goddamned gardener or the chauffeur or somebody like that. And she could've got anybody she wanted, too. She was a truly beautiful woman. She was wearing a silk blouse that showed off her big billowing bosom, and tight maroon slacks, and her hair—it was platinum blond now—was worn in an elegant upsweep. I'd have been satisifed to have half her good looks when I was her age.

It was a hot day and after lunch, with the sun climbing higher into the sky and burning it into an empty whiteness, everybody went swimming. We'd all brought swimsuits. I originally was going to wear a proper one-piece suit, but Charley told me to wear a bikini. I told him I didn't think it would be correct under the circumstances, but he insisted, saying, "If I can't have you, at least I can look at you."

So I brought along a white suit, which looked good against my tanned body. I put it on in one of the cabanas that stood alongside Charley's private beach and came strutting out with a towel around my shoulders. I timed it so I'd be the last one down to the beach. When I got to the crest of the grassy hill that sloped to the water people started looking up at me. You know, you really know, when you've landed right in the middle of somebody's eye, and I felt terrifically good and proud as I walked down to the beach. It isn't conceit but pride, pride in what you have.

Everybody was watching me; the men had their eyes riding up and down me and it felt like shock waves. (I wondered if any of Charley's friends knew what was going on. I suspected a few did, from the little, narrowed-eyed, *intimate* smiles I got from some of them, as if they had had descriptions of my snatch.) The ladies were more reserved in their appraisals, of course. Most of them were older than I, some of them in their thirties and forties, their big cans stuffed into their suits and rolls of fat bunched up around their shoulder straps.

Charley looked great in a swimsuit for a guy his age. He had broad shoulders and powerful arms and a big chest that was covered with gray-black hair. Helene was wearing a two-piece suit and, frankly, she shouldn't have. Her big bosom tended to sag and look groggy, and she had something of a belly, and there was some jelly flesh around her thighs. Nevertheless, sitting back in her beach chair, with her blond upswept hair and sunglasses, smoking a cigarette in a long holder, she looked elegant. She was the only one who didn't go in the water.

I swam out to the float in the middle of the water and hauled myself up onto it. Charley was the only other person to swim out that far. He came through the water—smoking a big cigar—heading for the float.

"Don't come up," I told him.

"Why not?" he asked, bobbing next to the float, the cigar in his mouth.

"She's watching us."

"So what?"

"Charley, please."

For once he listened to me. He stayed in the water.

"You look spectacular," he said.

"Thank you," I said. I wished he'd go away; I felt uncomfortable even talking to him. I knew she was watching us; I could feel it, and to know you're being watched from a distance is somehow more disturbing than being watched from close up.

"Listen," he said, "then get the hell off the float. I want to get up on it."

So I dove into the water, making a big splash around him.

"Hey, bitch!" he yelled. "You put my cigar out."

"I'll light you up all over tonight," I said, starting to swim back to shore.

"About midnight," he said.

Leave it to Charley to make a date for midnight. But okay, I'd be ready.

With him sitting on the float now, a lot of the men began swimming out there, like so many little fish following the big shark.

When I came out of the water a beach boy handed me a towel and I sat down on my blanket. I was about to stretch out in the sun to dry off when Helene walked over.

"Did you enjoy your swim?" she asked.

"It was great," I said.

She stood there staring down at me very thoughtfully. When it was starting to get to the point where I was feeling uncomfortable, she said, "Would you like to see the boat?"

"Oh, yes," I said. "I'd love to."

The boat was tied up at the private dock, about a hundred yards away.

"Come on, then," she said, turning and walking away.

I got up and followed her, the towel around my shoulders. I needed this like I needed another vagina. I'd already been on the boat, of course—eaten on it, showered on it, slept on it, got laid on it—but naturally I couldn't tell her that. I'm sure she didn't know *everything* that Charley and me did. So I had to remember to act excited and interested by everything, as if I was seeing it all for the first time.

From the way Helene began showing me around and explaining things once we were aboard, I knew she didn't know that I'd been there before. She showed me the enclosed upper deck, where the captain stood, and the wheel and the sextant and the ship-to-shore radio and things like that. Then she took me downstairs and showed me the kitchen (the galley, she called it) with its stove and refrigerator and the john with its shower, and the small living room with its fancy carpeting and color TV, and the guest room, and then the master bedroom. I pretended to be so excited, asking questions, saying how wonderful it was—which wasn't easy, since it was like old home week for me, especially that master bedroom.

"Would you like something to drink?" she asked when we'd sat down in the bedroom.

"No thanks," I said.

I was sitting on the edge of the bed (where I'd slept with Charley, for Christ's sake) and she was in a chair.

"Would you like to go cruising sometime?" she asked.

"I'd love to," I said. "Do you go out often?"

"Not too often," she said. She crossed her legs and her big white thighs got wider. You could tell she must have been a real stunner in her day—she still had good legs, with beautifully shaped calves, and that belly had no doubt been flat, and that bosom must have been blue ribbon.

"I'd practically live on this boat, if it were mine," I said.

She gave me a pinched little smile, as if to say, "You'll have to get your own boat, dearie; this one will never be yours." She took off her sunglasses, twirled them for a moment, and then put them down on a nearby table.

"So, Terry," she said, "how has life been treating you since last we met?"

"Fairly well," I said, hoping she wasn't going to get into anything heavy.

"It should. You're so young and beautiful."

"Why, thank you," I said, giving her my sweetest smile, saying to myself: Lord, please don't let her ask about Charley. I was a lousy liar, and I hated to lie—especially to someone who knew I was lying.

"I suppose I envy you," she said. "Having the world in front of you the way you do."

"Envy is for people who have regrets, Mrs. Corbett; and I don't suppose you have many of those."

She gave me a positively evil smile, clasping her fingers under her chin and lowering a gaze on me. I would have given fifty dollars right then and there to know the meaning of *that*.

"Well," I went on, "I just try to take it one day at a time."

"Don't waste any of it, Terry. Youth is like a faucet turning itself off very, very slowly—hardly noticeable at your age, but still turning nevertheless, all the time."

I didn't know what kind of half-assed philosophy that was supposed to be, but I nodded as if it was very deep.

"You can't believe when you're young that it's not going to last forever," she said.

I could believe it. I could feel myself aging by the second.

She got up, came across the carpeting, and sat down next to me on the bed.

"You're worldly but still innocent," she said, looking across her shoulder at me, her eyes searching mine. "Aren't you, Terry?"

"In what way, Mrs. Corbett?" I asked.

For an answer she put her arm around me, drew me close to her, and kissed me on the lips. Then she smiled. Her hand was moving slowly up and down my shoulder and arm.

"You're so sweet and beautiful," she whispered.

"I'm not so sweet, really," I said.

"And warm. You feel so warm."

She bent her head and kissed me right in the cleavage. I stared down at her bent, curving neck, where that platinum hair was sweeping up. Her lips lingered in my cleavage, nuzzling away. I began to feel queasy; I didn't like a woman doing that to me. That big, hot body of hers was beginning to tremble. Christ, I asked myself, what the hell is going on here? How do I get out of this?

"Mrs. Corbett . . ."

"Shhhh," she said, right into my boobs.

I wanted to push her away, but I was afraid to touch her.

Then she pulled away, lifting her head and gazing gravely at me. She had little wrinkles around her eyes and some pinched lines going into the corners of her mouth.

But her face was still beautiful, though way down deep in her eyes it was cold. She took my hand and, holding it tightly, pressed it against her breast. A big, forty-five-year-old breast, that's what I felt. I didn't move my fingers at all, but kept them stiff as little boards.

"I want you to relax," she whispered.

"Mrs. Corbett, I wish you wouldn't do this."

She continued to force my hand against her breast, staring me right in the eye.

"You don't know what you're talking about," she said. "You don't know what the world is all about. Terry, I want to help you."

She said this in a very soft, tense voice. But if she thought I didn't know what this was all about, she was crazy. Once, when I was still working, my sweet little fifty-year-old lady superviser invited me home to dinner and I went only because she was my boss and I figured she was lonely. But then, after dinner, when she told me she'd bought me some underwear and why didn't I try it on, and when she suggested that later we take a shower together, I knew I'd landed in another cockeyed corner of the world and got the hell out of there. Christ, and it was dirty old men my mother had always warned me about.

Now she let go of my hand and put her arms around me and tried to gather me in for a big kiss. I brought my arms up and pressed against that big sagging bosom to try and create a buffer between us, but she kept coming. Her weight forced me down onto my back and she was right on top of me, her hot wet lips on mine, kissing me with force and pressure. I tried to twist my head to a side but couldn't. She was, for God's sake, trying to soul-kiss, but I kept my lips clenched tight. I put my hands on her shoulders, appalled by the feel of that storming pent-up flesh, but couldn't budge her. It was scary, scary as hell, especially coming from this woman who seemed to have so much dignity, who seemed built and packed for men alone, who still had a body that could give a dead elephant a hard-on.

"Terry . . . Terry . . ." she said, as though trying to soothe me.

"Please, Mrs. Corbett," I said, "let me up. I ... I don't swing that way."

"I want you to relax ... please ... don't be frightened."

"I don't like this," I said.

"You don't know anything about it."

"But I'm not ... I don't ..." Christ, I didn't even know what to *say*.

She kept me down by the force of her weight. A couple of times her hand dropped onto my thigh and started wandering between my legs, but each time I was able to push it away. I didn't know what to do. I couldn't very well start screaming and have people come in and find us there like that, and neither did I want to get *too* violent.

"Please let me up," I said. My view of the world was confined at that moment to down the top of her bathing suit, to where her boobs were white.

She was stronger than I was, the bitch, and she was in heat, panting into my face. Somehow she got both my arms up over my head and pinned them at the wrists with one hand. Then her other hand dropped out of sight and the next thing I knew it was at the knot holding together the lower half of my bikini. Now I really started to fight back, kicking and struggling as best I could. She drew herself up on top of me, straddling me with both knees, those big folded-back white thighs staring me in the face like a couple of ski slopes. She was panting, her mouth was open, her lower lip hanging. She kept fussing at the knot, grimacing and panting, until it came undone, and then with a strong tug she pulled the damn thing right off me.

"Oh, shit, Mrs. Corbett!" I yelled, trying to clamp my legs together, half naked now and really getting scared.

"Be quiet, be quiet," she said in a furious whisper, sounding not like she was worried about anyone hearing, but more like she was irritated, as if I was disturbing her concentration. Now she was trying to get her hand under my back to reach my halter knot. It wasn't easy for her because she was still using one hand to keep my arms pinned, and I was wriggling and squirming like a hooked fish. But she did it; the goddamned bitch did it with a very fierce and determined show of strength that was scary.

When she had my halter off she bent forward and started sucking on my breasts. She was getting all worked up, breathless and moaning. And me lying under her stark naked, like prime cut.

"Mrs. Corbett," I said, "let me up."

"Be quiet," she whispered.

For about five minutes she played with my breasts, kissing them and sucking on them and fingering the nipples and holding them against her face, that creamy platinum hair bobbing around under my eyes. Then she began kissing my stomach, and slowly her kisses were going lower and lower. I knew where she was heading, but I wasn't fighting it anymore, even after she let go of my arms. Once I tried to sit up but she looked at me like she was startled, her eyes almost appealing, as if begging me not to move, as if she had traveled some great distance and worked so hard for this. So I fell back down again, feeling caught and helpless. I closed my eyes, as if that was my way of saying that I didn't want to have anything to do with it.

With her strong hands she pulled me forward until my legs were spread at the edge of the bed; then she got down to the floor and sank to her knees and started probing and massaging with her fingers. I didn't like the feel of her in there and started to cross my legs.

"Don't," I said.

"Be still, be still," she said, her voice running with breathless tension.

And for a moment I lost track of what was going on. Her involvement was so intense and single-minded it was almost as if she was having a religious experience, and she was able to communicate that feeling to me, that this was somehow holy and sacred and I had better not do anything to upset it. And besides, I was scared; there wasn't a hell of a lot I could do to get out of this without spilling some mighty sour apples. Also, she was so goddamned thoroughly worked up and determined that I was afraid she might be violent if I tried to stop her. She looked like she was in a trance as she sat there fingering me and kissing my curly tangle of pubics.

When she pressed forward and went in with her tongue I gave a little yelp and was suddenly shot through with tension that felt like it was stretching every nerve and paralyzing every muscle. I had known she was going to do it, but somehow I couldn't believe it until it actually happened: I couldn't believe that this beautiful and statuesque woman with the platinum blond hair and all the money and all the dignity was going down on me.

My God, but I knew it wasn't the first time she was doing this. She was so hot and smooth, she knew exactly what she was doing. I felt like I was being invaded, right into my soul. I was straining to meet her halfway and get it over with as quickly as possible, but she was taking her time; I could hear every soft wet licking sound of it. I was trying my damnedest to stay uninvolved, but it was becoming a losing struggle. The whole mad erotic tone of it began to get to me and I felt the tension starting to ease and to feel, really *feel* what she was doing. There was nothing hard or fierce about her now; she was positively tender, even loving. This was bliss for her, and she seemed to have an instinct for what I was feeling, what I wanted—more than any man had ever shown me.

It happened all of a sudden, with a rush that made the room turn around in circles and left me dizzy; and she knew how to keep it going, keep that tide flowing, how much pressure to put and when and where. She was moaning, we were both moaning; if anybody had been listening, God forbid, they wouldn't have been able to tell if they were hearing sounds of misery or ecstasy. When it began to play itself out she seemed to lose her cool and applied more pressure, going faster and faster, like a dog lapping up water. She kept going even after I had stopped reacting, and then finally she stopped.

I rolled over on the bed and curled myself up, exhausted, drained, trying to catch my breath. I don't think I had a thought in my head—I was just staring into space, aware now that the boat was rocking gently and that I could hear faint laughter coming from the party. I had a sick feeling at the pit of my stomach.

I felt a pressure on the other side of the bed and knew

she was lying next to me. She began caressing my ass and I pulled away; I didnt want the bitch near me, much less touching me.

"How do you feel, darling?" she asked.

"Is this how you get your kicks?" I asked.

"I asked you how you felt."

"Lousy."

"But you enjoyed it, didn't you?"

"No," I said sourly. "I want to get the hell out of here."

"Soon."

She was moving around on the bed and when I turned to see what she was doing now I found she had removed the top of her bathing suit and was up on her knees, beginning to pull down the bottom half of her suit.

"Oh, no!" I yelled, getting off the other side of the bed and jumping to my feet.

She seemed puzzled, kneeling there on the bed with her big breasts hanging with their enormous flat red nipples, her thumbs inside the top of her suit, which she had pulled down just far enough so that the deep incurving folds of her sex area showed and just a little bit of pubic hair—enough to show she wasn't a platinum blond, not that I'd had any doubts.

"Why not, Terry?"

"Why not?" I yelled. "Do I need a goddamned reason?"

Standing there naked like that, I began feeling angry. I had visions of her pinning me again and forcing her big fat snatch into my face. All I wanted was to get out of there, fast. I think she must have sensed that it had gone far enough, that nothing else was going to happen, that I was good and mad now, and that anyway there were some forms of sexual assault that were harder to accomplish than others.

She watched me pick up my bikini and put it on (next time I was alone with this bitch I'd wear a suit of armor). Then I grabbed my towel and threw it around my neck as haughtily as though it were a mink wrap.

She still hadn't moved, was kneeling there, looking now like she was holding her pants up. There was genuine pained disappointment in her face, almost disbelief in her eyes as she watched me hurry the hell out of there.

When I got up on the deck the fresh air felt delicious. I stood at the railing for a moment, trying to compose myself. Then I climbed off of the boat onto the dock. I looked back for a moment, wondering what she was doing in there by herself. I think I had a pretty good idea. Then I headed back to the beach.

There weren't too many people still out by the water. Charley was sitting on a beach chair talking to some men and when he caught sight of me hurrying along, looking all bedraggled and beat up (that's how I *felt*, anyway), he watched me like a hawk. When I neared him he took off his sunglasses and gave me a look that I read as sad and sympathetic. I stared him right in the eye as I passed and his eyes dropped and he turned his head aside.

The son of a bitch knew.

Chapter Eight

"You're goddamned wife is a *pervert!*" I screamed at him. "A goddamned pervert! She's crazy. She's out of her *mind!* She stripped me down and went at me like a goddamned St. Bernard, while you were soaking your ass in Long Island Sound with your friends."

I was really letting him have it, and the more he just sat there looking miserably unhappy, the more I poured it on; it was as if I was taking advantage of the opportunity to yell at him, to hear the top of my voice in his presence. Or maybe it was just the need to let off some steam. The ride back had been just great, me sitting and boiling and Frankie the Mummy at the wheel, me having to hold it all back during the long drive.

The first thing I did when I got home was take a shower—just stand under the hottest water I could bear and keep soaping up my you-know-what to get rid of the stink of that woman. Then I turned off all the lights and stood naked in front of an open window to air out, letting the soft night breezes run against me. The more I thought about it the more furious I got. To be raped by a woman! I was sorry I hadn't put my knee someplace where she'd never forget. The son of a bitch. She knew she had me dead to rights, that I couldn't make a fuss. Talk about all in the family. I wouldn't have been surprised now to hear that they wanted to adopt me, I was so much fun.

And Charley knew, the bastard. At first I had wondered if I ought to talk to him about it, but I wiped that doubt away without any trouble. You'd better talk to him, I told myself, let him know what you had to put up with.

So I laced it into him for about twenty minutes, walking back and forth in my bathrobe. He felt bad, there was no question about that—otherwise he would never have let me carry on the way I did. He just sat slumped in an easy chair, his head in his hand, his eyes following me around the room.

"She's not a pervert," he interjected while I drew a breath.

I glared at him.

"Oh, no?" I asked. "I suppose what she did is approved by Good Housekeeping. What do you mean she's not a pervert?"

"It very seldom happens."

"Don't tell me I'm supposed to be *flattered* that she picked on me? And anyway, how do you know what she does? Does she know what you do? Does she know about us?"

"I don't know."

"You bet your ass she does. That's why she did it. To get even."

"With who?" he asked, giving a grunting laugh.

I put my hands on my hips and stared at him. He had the most sorrowful look.

"Charley," I said, a bit toned down now, "how long has it been going on?"

"Not more than a few years, I don't think. We had a maid that quit, and I wanted to know why. I like to stay informed about those things, you know. Well, it developed that Helene was ... was after her. You know what I mean."

"Do I know what you mean!" I asked and gave him a sarcastic laugh. "Listen, Charley, does she have affairs with men?"

He scowled.

"She'd better not," he said. "She knows better, and so does all of mankind."

"So that's how she gets her kicks. Christ, so that's why you wanted me out there in my little bikini."

"That's a lotta crap," he said. He was mad now.

"You brought me out there like a sacrifice to the gods."

"Terry, you say that again and I'll slap you around." He was good and mad now. "That's like calling *me* a pervert."

"Do you think she's jealous of me?"

71

"How the hell do I know what's in her head?"

"She's your wife."

"We don't communicate very much."

"Don't you ever discuss her problem?"

"What problem?" he asked.

"What she did to me," I yelled. "Charley, she's got a problem, for Christ's *sake*."

"She doesn't know that I know."

"But aren't you concerned?"

"There's nothing I can do about it," he said.

"At least you could've warned me about her."

"How do you warn about something like that?"

"What did you think when you saw us walking off together?"

"I didn't see you going," he said. "Later I asked somebody where Helene was and they said she was showing the boat to the broad in the bikini, which was you. That's when I knew what was happening, because Helene hates the boat—she wouldn't want to show it to anybody."

"She hates the boat?"

"Because I never take her out on it. Leave me alone, Terry, for Christ's sake. I come here to relax, not to stir up aggravation."

"She must be very lonely," I said thoughtfully, pinching my lower lip. Then, "Crap, I caught myself almost feeling sorry for her."

"Don't," he said. "Don't ever feel sorry for anybody."

"I'll bet she was beautiful once."

"She was a bathing beauty, won all sorts of contests."

"Now she's getting old."

"She worries about it too much. She's always going to the beauty parlor and doing this and that to her hair, and soaking herself and oiling herself and powdering herself. She thinks it's a crime to get old. I tell her to think of all the people who die young; she's got it over them anyway."

"Charley, can I ask you a personal question?"

"I know what you're going to ask," he said pointing his finger at me, "and it's none of your goddamned business."

"But you're home *some*times . . . doesn't she ever . . ."

"You're getting out of line, Terry," he said, shaking that finger.

"I'm sorry," I said. "You're right. It's none of my business. But do me a favor, huh? Don't invite me out there anymore. I don't want to be near her."

"Don't worry," he said. "I won't make that mistake again. I got a phobia against people doing what I don't want them to do."

He wasn't lying about that, I can tell you.

I always felt there would never have been any trouble between Charley and me if only other people would have kept out of things. We continued to get along great. Despite the difference in our ages, he never treated me like a daughter or a kid sister or anything like that. He treated me like a woman, and he knew how to do it. We continued to travel, to all the right places at all the right times, and to go to the good clubs and restaurants. And sometimes he'd come in and just take off his shoes and jacket and, exhausted, lie down on the couch and take a nap—just like a regular guy coming home from work. On those nights I'd knock together a little dinner, nothing fancy (I was *not* the world's best cook—I could barely get a steak in and out of the oven without turning it to canvas), and we'd spend the night sitting in front of the TV.

I think the biggest compliment he ever paid me was when he brought that guy Bruno up to the apartment one night. I didn't know who Bruno was, except that he was some big, cannon-sized pistol from France who Charley treated with the kind of respect he never showed anybody else. Charley phoned and told me he was bringing a friend up for "drinks and talk," and that I should tidy up the place, make sure there was booze and ice, and to dress "nice but not flashy." It was the first time he ever brought anybody up there, so I knew it had to be something special.

Well, Bruno didn't look like anybody special. He was a little man with round dark eyes that looked like they'd been fouled by something sick in his brain, and between his nose and upper lip was a broad space that gave him the appearance of an ape. But he had perfect manners; he spoke very quietly and when he shook my hand he held the tips of my fingers and bowed his head like a goddamned ambassador or something.

There were two other men—one a friend of Bruno's, a real sphinx, and a friend of Charley's, Petey, whose girl friend I had met a few times while out with Charley. Her name was Gloria. She was a pea-brained redhead who described herself as Petey's "tootsie" (I didn't think people talked like that anymore) and confided to me once that Petey sometimes shot people. I didn't even hear her.

Petey helped me make the drinks, while Bruno's sphinx lounged in the doorway with his arms crossed watching us, as if he didn't trust us. Then, after about ten minutes of polite conversation, during which Bruno invited Charley and me to Paris, Charley said, "Terry, your TV program is on now."

I knew what he meant. I excused myself, went into the bedroom and closed the door, and put on the TV and turned it up loud enough so they knew I couldn't overhear. And believe me, I wasn't even interested. I just sat there with the blasting TV, thinking how nice it was to have company in the apartment for a change, even if it was only Bruno, who looked like an ape, his friend the sphinx, and Petey, who sometimes shot people (which I didn't believe, of course; I was a champ at brainwashing myself in those days).

That was the evening and at one o'clock in the morning Charley came into the bedroom and said they were gone. And that was the whole evening, as far as I was concerned.

Chapter Nine

But my troubles started right after that. I had never thought about trouble, even though I knew Charley operated on the shady side of life. Charley always seemed so relaxed, living just the way he wanted, smiling and scowling behind his big cigar. And while he had friends like big Petey the shooter and gorillas like Big Stoney hanging around, he was also always introducing me to big-name show people and politicians and judges and lawyers and other characters who would be the pride of any neighborhood. It turned out to be that S.O.B. Bruno who carried the plague.

About a week after Bruno's visit Charley took off to San Juan on a short business trip. He would do that now and then—go somewhere without me. I never asked any questions, of course. He never stayed away longer than two or three days and always brought me back a present. Most of the time these short hops were to Puerto Rico, but once he went to Bogotá, Colombia. He would tell me he'd be gone for a few days and that I should miss him, which I did. Everything seemed to come to a standstill when Charley wasn't around, even big, nonstop, swinging New York.

The first night he was away I stayed home, watching TV. But the second night I started to feel a little stir crazy and went out to a movie. The picture let out at midnight, and because the theater was just a few blocks from the apartment I decided to walk. The block between Third Avenue and Second was dark and empty when I turned the corner. It looked like a long, spooky corridor.

I became aware of the car when I was about halfway into the block. It was following me very slowly, hardly making a sound, like it had a kitten under the hood instead of an engine. I didn't turn around but kept walking at the same pace, trying to look confident and unconcerned, but staying alert, and starting to get scared. I thought about going into the next building (there was a row of brownstones) and making believe I lived there, except that if somebody was really after me they'd catch me in the vestibule, since I didn't have a key to go anyplace. Then I thought to myself that maybe it was just somebody looking for an address or a parking space. But that was just wishful thinking; whoever was in that car was up to no good—my New Yorker's instincts told me that. I wished somebody else was on the street, even a little old lady walking her schnauzer. Then the car pulled ahead of me and I couldn't help but look at it. There were two guys in it, both of them looking at me, and all I could think was: Oh, you dumb thrill-seeking crumbs, if Charley saw this he'd kill you. Then the car stopped, in the middle of the street, both doors opened, and the two guys got out, leaving the doors open and the inside of the car lit up.

I stopped. My first thought was to turn around and start running; my second was to stay there and start screaming if they tried anything. They walked between two parked cars, stepped up onto the sidewalk and headed for me. I watched them. They seemed to be in their late twenties and didn't *look* like bad guys, if that means anything. They were wearing short windbreakers, unzipped, sport shirts, beat-up khakis. When they got closer I saw they had pretty tough faces, the kind that didn't smile easily.

"What's this all about?" I asked.

And then, to my amazement, I heard a voice come from somewhere asking the same thing: "Yeah. What's it all about?"

I looked and so did they. To my surprise and relief and delight, there was a guy sitting on the top step of a brownstone. The three of us looked at him. He got up slowly and began coming down the steps. He was a kid, about nineteen or so, with hair down to his shoulders and a short beard. He was sturdily built and looked like he could take care of himself.

I couldn't believe it. In New York City—somebody

willing to get involved, willing to help. The one guy in a million.

The two guys waited for him to get to the sidewalk and then one of them walked up to him and I was all ready for the swingout, prepared to pitch in and help any way I could.

Then one of the guys said to the kid, "Thoughtful of you, buddy, but we're police officers."

I believed it, but the kid didn't, though he wasn't entirely sure. He shot a glance at me, as if to say, "Who are you anyway, babe, and what's going on?" There are few things tougher than being a good Samaritan in New York City.

The cop took out some I.D., flashed it at the kid, then said, "Okay? Now take a walk."

Now the kid gave me an outright dirty look, as if I'd been setting him up or something. One minute he was ready to bleed for me, and the next he writes me off as some kind of degenerate, just because a civil servant shows him a badge. I thought kids today were sharper than that. But he just sauntered off into the night, his hands in his pockets. He didn't look back.

"How about going for a spin around the block, Terry?" one of the cops said.

They even knew my name. I didn't like them. They seemed too cocky and wise-assed. I had never thought about the cops; Charley wasn't too crazy about them ("There are some good ones, but not many," he'd say), but I never gave them much thought one way or the other.

"You guys arresting me?" I asked.

And I'll tell you something: I got the most peculiar feeling, right then and there—something that had nothing to do with anything but myself. I had always been respectful of the police; I had been brought up that way and taught that way and honestly believed that way. Like most people, I was respectful and even a little afraid of real authority. But all of a sudden it struck me that I was not respectful or afraid, but was instead feeling a sharp resentment toward and dislike for these guys; they were suddenly the *enemy* to me. And while I naturally didn't take the time to think about it in any deep way at that moment, I realized that somewhere along the way I had, without knowing it, *changed*.

"We just want to talk to you," the cop said.

"For a little while," the other one said.

"What about?" I asked.

"Get in the car and find out."

"No," I said.

"It's about Charley."

"What about him?" I asked, getting a little nervous.

"Come on, Terry," one of them said in a confidential, cajoling voice. "We can't talk out here in the street."

All of my instincts said no, but instincts are a pushover for curiosity. I wondered what Charley would have wanted me to do. Maybe these guys were two of his "Christmas" cops (it was always Christmas when they came around, he used to say) and they wanted to get a message to him. They sure as hell knew who I was—at least they weren't being cute about anything. And maybe something had happened to Charley, maybe he was in some kind of trouble. (That was my ego talking; if Charley was in any kind of trouble he had a battery of highly paid legal eagles who would have been the first to know. But the thought actually occurred to me that if Charley was in trouble he, or somebody, wanted to let me know, as if I could do anything about it. Christ, were my brains bent!)

So, with all the best of intentions, I got into the car, sitting in the front seat between two cops. We went to Second Avenue then downtown. We didn't go anyplace in particular—just cruised in and out of side streets on the East Side while they tried to get information out of me. I realized after a few minutes that that was what it was— the cops were fishing.

The one on my right did most of the asking, while the one at the wheel was pretty quiet. The wise bastards, when I asked them what their names were, said Death and Taxes. Death was doing the driving, the quiet one. Taxes offered me a cigarette, which I refused.

"Where's Charley?" Taxes asked as soon as we turned our first corner.

"I have no idea," I said.

"Why'd he go to San Juan?"

"Look, if you knew he went to San Juan why'd you ask me where he was?"

"We're trying to find out if you're going to be helpful," Taxes said.

"I love being helpful," I said, "but I don't know anything."

"What's Charley do for a living?"

"I haven't the slightest."

"Terry," Taxes said, "you're with the guy three, four days a week; are you trying to tell us you don't know how he makes a buck?"

"I'm telling you the truth," I said.

Now Death sighed. A sigh from a quiet person is scary.

"Forgive us, Terry," he said. "We're cops. We so seldom hear the truth we can't recognize it anymore."

"Then maybe you'd better let me off at the next corner," I said.

"Just take it easy, Terry," Taxes said, "Look, when we talk about you being helpful, it's for yourself as well as us. You could be in pretty deep trouble."

"For what?" I asked, looking at him.

"Oh," he said casually, turning his face toward the window, "aiding and abetting, being an accessory, withholding information, lying to a police officer."

"You don't lie unless you're under oath," I said, trying to say what I meant, but not meaning what I was saying, getting a little confused.

Death laughed—a mean, snickering sound.

"That's the time to lie all right," he said.

"If you tell us what you know, Terry," Taxes said, "you'll be helping yourself one hell of a lot, I can assure you."

"But I don't know anything," I said.

We were going up Third Avenue now, cruising slowly in the right-hand lane. The traffic was light and there weren't many people on the streets. I spotted two young ladies of the evening on the corner in their mini-skirts and knee-length leather boots.

"Look," I said, pointing to them, "there's two hookers. Why don't you arrest them and stop annoying honest citizens?"

Both cops glanced indifferently at the hookers.

"Terry," Taxes said, looking back to me, "don't say you don't know anything. You might be being honest and *think* you don't know anything; but you'd be surprised as hell at how much you *do* know."

"Look," I said, "I know you guys are trying to do your job, whatever it is; but I'm not trying to jive you—I really *don't* know anything."

"Why did Charley go to Vegas last March?" he asked.

"I don't know," I said.

"You went with him, didn't you?"

"Sure, but I don't know why he went."

"Who'd you see out there?"

"Nobody."

"Why did Charley go to L.A. in June?"

"Don't ask me," I said.

"I am asking you," Taxes said.

I just kept staring through the windshield, staring with dumb innocence at Third Avenue, Second Avenue, various side streets.

"You mean to say," Taxes went on, "that he just told you that you were going to L.A. and you didn't ask him why?"

"That's right," I said.

They didn't say anything for about five minutes after that. I figured I had stymied them. Then Death said, "You ever meet a guy named Bruno Sorel?"

I had to think for a second; this was the first question they'd asked that I could answer. I bit my lip.

"No," I said.

"Weren't you home when Charley brought him up to your place recently?" Taxes asked.

"I don't know any Brunos," I said.

Telling the lie, the first real lie, made me feel uncomfortable, and a little scared, too.

"Where were you the night Charley brought him up?" Taxes asked.

"I'm there every night," I said. "I never met anybody named Bruno."

"Maybe he used a different name," Death said.

"That's right," Taxes said. "Maybe he did. He's a little guy, talks with a French accent..."

And looks like an ape, I thought.

"Charley never brought anybody up to the apartment," I said. "Listen, how about taking me home, huh?"

"Soon," Taxes said. "You hear much of their conversation?"

"If I never met the guy..." I said.

"You know what he does for a living?" Taxes asked.

I didn't say anything. I didn't know what Bruno the ape did for a living and sure as hell didn't want to.

"He's Charley's connection on the hard stuff," Taxes said.

I was quiet. Then Death said, "Or didn't you know what Charley-boy does for a living?"

"I don't know anything," I said, oh so softly. My head was beginning to spin. What the hell were they telling me this crap for? I didn't want to know about it. But my head was being jarred; it was as if some information which I had been successfully suppressing way down deep for a long time had suddenly ripped loose and was going through my head like a hurricane. *Didn't you suspect that, Terry?* I asked myself. *Didn't you really suspect it was something like that and been ignoring it, trying to cover it up? Come on, Terry, what have you been hiding from yourself, for the sake of the good life and staying out of the subway?* I clenched my fists, and don't think those bastards didn't notice.

"Charley's not in a nice business," Taxes said.

"Charley's not a nice guy," Death said.

"I don't know anything," I said, hardly able to talk above a whisper.

"Would you like to come over to the station and tell some people what you don't know?" Taxes asked.

"I want to go home."

"You can help yourself if you'll cooperate," Taxes said.

"There's nothing I can tell you," I said, beginning to

wonder where it all went from here. Why did these bastards have to *tell* me?

"Look, Terry," Taxes said, "*we* know you're just a plain kid from the Bronx, and maybe *we* believe you; but there are some other people who might not be so trusting. Some people look upon the distribution of heroin mighty seriously."

"Please take me home," I said. "I don't know anything."

They stopped bugging me then and drove me home. They didn't say another word. When they pulled up in front of my building Taxes got out and stood aside with the open door and let me out. I waited for him to say some last thing, some word of warning or advice, or even good night. But he didn't say anything; he didn't even look at me. He simply got back into the car, closed the door, and they drove away. I stood on the sidewalk watching them go, watched them pause at the corner, taillight pulsing to show the direction of their turn, and then make the turn and disappear.

I was good and scared. I hung around the apartment the next few days, a real nail-biter. I couldn't eat, couldn't sleep. I didn't leave the apartment for a minute, not wanting to miss Charley's call. I couldn't wait to see him again, to tell him what had happened. I wouldn't tell him anything on the phone—maybe it was being tapped (boy, you can get paranoid in a hurry)—but tell him to get right over there.

He had said he would be away for just a few days. But a week went by with no word. I started to get panicky. Maybe he had been picked up, maybe what had happened to me was an indication that something was going on. I had the doorman bring up the paper each morning and I read it from cover to cover, looking for some news about Charley. I knew that if he got arrested it would be news. But there was nothing. Nothing in the paper, nothing on the phone. It got so bad that one night I was even tempted to call Helene, to see if she had heard from Charley. I didn't, of course, but even to think about it shows how much of a shaking my nerves were taking.

And then one night the doorbell rang. I figured it had to be Charley. I got so excited I actually ran across the living room to let him in. But when I opened the door it was those two friends of his who I had seen from time to time, Mac and Big Stoney. They were standing in the doorway staring at me from way back deep in their eyes, and Big Stoney was carrying that suitcase. Charley wanted to see me in Jersey, they said.

Chapter Ten

I don't know for how long I lay in that busted-up car, pinned down by a dead man. After a little while I realized the car was resting on its side, and it took me some time, too, to realize the windshield was gone, blasted out by Big Stoney's hurtling body. Mac was lying across me as if he didn't have a bone in his body, his head resting on my chest, one arm hanging. I was too scared to move, as if I might somehow bring him back to life if I did. I think I was prepared to lie there like that forever, if it was the only way for me to live—that's how much living can suddenly mean to you.

I had a dull throbbing pain in my head, where I might have knocked it against something during the crash. But I don't think I ever lost consciousness. I guess I had been afraid to. After all, they had tried to kill me. These bastards had actually tried to kill me. The deeper the thought sank, the more upset I got. It was a horrible thought—that somebody wanted to see you dead, was prepared to do it, had actually been in the act of making it happen. I think I started to cry. *Wait till Charley finds out about* ... But I never finished the thought. Because Charley was the one who had sent them. It was like a corkscrew going through my guts, making itself felt and believed.

I remembered the line now, those words. I think it was about a year before. We were sitting in a restaurant in Greenwich Village, Charley and me and some hard-faced friends of his. They were talking about somebody they obviously didn't like and one of the guys said, "I'd like to see him in Jersey." On the way home I asked Charley what that meant. I remember I was drowsy and hardly paying attention, sort of just trying to make conversation.

Charley's answer was that sometimes when there was trouble and somebody had to be taken care of (I didn't ask what *that* meant), they often left the person in some shadowy place in New Jersey (it was one of the few times he ever told me anything of that nature). Wanting to see somebody in Jersey meant.... I goddamned well knew what it meant now.

I gathered my strength and by pushing up with both hands began clearing Mac off of me. It's true what they say about deadweight: he felt like he weighed a ton. What I had to do was push him aside and slide out from under him. It wasn't easy—dead people seem to want to stay put. Then I saw that bullet hole over his right temple. I think it was the sight of that that snapped me back to reality (or as real as this messy goddamned situation could be). It struck me then that Mac was really dead, that the bullet had been intended for me, and that when I hit Big Stoney's hand the shot had gone wild, Mac's foot had frozen on the accelerator and... Boy, that was a brilliant deduction, what with him lying on top of me with that hole drilled in his head.

At first I tried to free myself as gently as possible—still with that fear of waking him up, I guess, as absurd as that was. But then, making very little progress, I thrust as hard as I could and, holding his flopping body back with one hand, managed to slide free.

With the car lying on its side, I was going to have to get out through the window (I could have got out through the windshield, but the glass was very jagged and I didn't want to chance it). As I made my way up toward the window I bumped into something. It was that suitcase Big Stoney had been carrying. Since I had been curious about the damned thing, I picked it up and tossed it out ahead of me. I found my purse, too, and tossed that out. Then I stood up, took hold of the sides of the window, and hoisted myself out. I sat on the door for a second, looking around at where I was. I was nowhere. The car had shot off of the road and landed a good fifty feet or so in the woods. And that's all there was—woods and more woods, with just enough light from a half-moon to show it off.

There wasn't a sound either; I guess the flying car had scared the crickets shitless.

When I slid down from the door I stepped back and looked at the car. It looked angry, lying there with its tires all stuck out the wrong way. Damned good thing it hadn't caught fire or exploded or anything like that. There would have been one overdone Terry if it had.

I wondered about Big Stoney. Could the big gorilla have survived? Guys in the circus were always being shot out of cannons in the afternoon and having dinner at night. But they didn't have to go through windshields and had a net waiting for them at the end of the trip. But the thought of Big Stoney being alive somewhere there in the dark, limping around with a carved-up face, turned my blood cold. I stood absolutely still, listening. The only thing I heard was a whisper of wind in the leaves.

I tried to figure out in which direction he might have gone, but I couldn't remember just when he had made his abrupt departure or which way the car was pointed at the time. But he couldn't have lived through that, even though he looked like he'd been born through the cross-breeding of an ox and a gorilla. And anyway, what was the point of looking for him? Suppose I found him? Suppose he was still alive? What the hell was I supposed to do—nurse him back to health? Screw you, Big Stoney, I thought, you who were one-tenth of a second from blasting my head to pieces.

I picked up my purse and began heading for the road, beginning to tremble now, the idea of how close it had all come—the bullet, the crashing car—really hitting me now. Christ, was death that casual a business, such an indifferent hit or miss? I'd always been taught that it was a great big thing with a lot of dignity.

But then something cut right through these high-toned thoughts like the edge of a knife: the suitcase. Wondering why that should be bugging me at that moment, I went back for it and picked it up. It wasn't too heavy. I put it down on the door of the overturned car and snapped it open, having to satisfy my damned curiosity once and for all. I took one look and closed it right away. Holy crap, I thought. It was all just lying in there, as neatly packed as if it had been put in by little old ladies, each packet wrapped around by a rubber band. There had to be thousands in there—tens of thousands, hundreds of thousands. Charley never dealt in chicken feed. Not my sweet, everlovin', good-natured Charley. Which, I wondered, was the evening's important job—delivering the money or getting rid of me? Need I ask. Money was money, the sturdy friend, the golden key; but a broad is just somebody to be dumped this week and replaced the next. So after leaving me somewhere to feed the squirrels, these bastards were going to drop the money with Charley. All part of the night's work: get the money, pick up Terry, blow her brains out, dump her, deliver the money, then go have a beer.

I'd seen those suitcases before; Charley occasionally parked one in the apartment overnight. No doubt they contained money (or maybe sometimes they contained the goods; and wouldn't that have been cute—me sleeping in the same room with a few million dollars' worth of heroin? Boy oh boy oh boy, how many centuries in jail do you get for that?). He really must have trusted me at one time, sweet Charley.

But what the hell was I going to do with it? What good was it going to do me? I thought about leaving it there, as if to show them I was really a good girl—sort of like a bribe—show them I was honest and they would let me live. Sure. For how long? Long enough to laugh in my face and send for somebody with greater efficiency at erasing the unwanted. Then I thought I ought to burn it. That would have been lovely. I had nowhere to go, they were really going to be out after me now; the least I could do was burn their goddamned money.

But nobody does that.

So I hauled the suitcase with me, knowing that no matter what, the first chance I got I was going to sit down and count it. There's something about money that makes you forget about reality.

As I worked my way through the dark underbrush I stumbled over something, nearly losing my footing. I looked down and shuddered. That answered the question about Big Stoney. He was lying in the grass, stretched out straight as a board. It was as if, flying through the air, he had suddenly hit an air pocket and dropped straight down. He was lying on his face (he always looked better when you couldn't see his face) and there were long rips and gashes down the back of his coat, carved in there by the windshield as he made his exit. But the funny thing—if anything was funny anymore—was his hat: he was still wearing it, but the crown was driven down tight across his head, and the brim was down too, over his ears, the way you'd put it on if you were trying for laughs at a dull party.

When I reached the road I felt pretty lonely—I didn't even have the dead for company anymore. I had no idea where I was, but that didn't seem to make any difference. The unkind idea of living on borrowed time had settled in on me now. Twice within a few seconds I had missed death by fractions. That sort of joy takes its toll. I remembered seeing a war movie once, when I was a kid (how long ago was that?), about these soldiers going through battle after battle, and after each survival coming out feeling a little less convinced about life. What was the word? Fatalistic. That was it. That was just about how I felt now. I was a combat veteran and each minute, each breath was like a bonus.

What I did was follow the road in the direction we had been going. I did that for two reasons: One, I couldn't remember passing anything back there for a while, and two, the road was going slightly downhill, which made it easier for me and my jackpot suitcase.

I walked for about half a mile, passing nothing but more woods, going through a neighborhood that I'll bet not even Daniel Boone ever saw, until I came to a main drag—at least it looked like a main drag compared to what I'd been traveling over. What it was was a two-lane highway, with some houses scattered back from the road. Up ahead were the lights of a roadside place. To me it looked like Times Square.

It was called Barney's Eats and Drinks and was probably the big action place around there. It was a restaurant with a bar. When I walked in everybody at the bar turned to look at me, all four of them. The four were men, and there's nothing like the slow, shameless once-over you get from rubes. They turned completely around and leaned back on the bar on their elbows, like a notice from each one that he had a pecker.

"The restaurant open?" I asked the bartender.

"For you it is, honey," he said.

For other people, too, apparently. There were a few couples at the tables, all sitting there quietly, as if they hated each other. I asked the waitress where the ladies room was. I followed her directions and headed for it. It was a one-stall johnny, with a cracked mirror and a thin stream of water running from the sink faucet.

I locked the door, went into the stall, locked that door and sat down and peed so long it's a wonder I didn't dehydrate. I'm surprised my kidneys hadn't come floating up into my throat.

Then I pulled the suitcase up onto my lap and opened it. The money looked even better in the light. Money like that, and I mean a whole lot of it, has a dignified look. It also looks cold, as if it's saying, I'm not really yours; yesterday I was somebody else's, tomorrow I'll be somebody else's. But right now it was mine, and so I counted it. It was in fifties and hundreds, with some twenties scattered here and there. I counted a dozen or so packages and each added up to five thousand. I stopped counting each bill and instead counted packages; it was easier that way. There were a hundred packages. Five hundred thousand dollars. A half million.

I was sitting on the bowl in Barney's Eats and Drinks with a half million dollars in my lap. Hardly a drop in anybody's bucket, not even Charley's.

I took one package, put it in my purse, closed the suitcase, pulled up my blue jeans, gave Barney's the courtesy of a flush, and stepped out of the stall. I combed my hair, washed away some of the smudges left by near death, and went back outside.

I thought of having a meal, but my stomach was still

too high-flying for that, so I went back to the bar, put my suitcase down, and sat on a stool—interrupting a hot baseball discussion among the bartender and the locals. The four guys got deadly quiet as the bartender came over, bar rag in hand. He gave the bar a good mopping, put down a coaster and napkin, and gave me a smile. He was a skinny little guy with a crew cut, smiling like people do when the TV camera picks them up on one of those afternoon game shows.

"Bourbon, neat," I said.

"Yes, ma'am," he said, like he was impressed. And I'm sure he was. Here in out of the night walks this young piece in the tightest blue jeans and tightest sweater he ever saw and orders bourbon neat ... and pays for it with a twenty no less.

The four guys never took their eyes off my boobs, but I didn't give a damn. I was used to that; I always had big breasts, from the time I was fourteen. For some reason my parents used to think I was immoral because of it. "Do you have to go out with so much in your sweater?" my mother would yell. (What she meant was I shouldn't show them off like that.) "What do you want me to do?" I'd ask. "Go down to the butcher and have him trim them?" Good God, what memories.

The booze was what I needed to settle me. I had to do some thinking now, real thinking, for the first time in my life practially. I wasn't just out on my own, I was walking around with a bull's-eye on me. I wondered when Charley would begin to suspect that something got fouled up, that the chipmunks weren't nibbling my ears. I wondered when the wreck would be found, with its two loveables. And I wondered where I ought to go, what I ought to do and if there was anybody in the world I could trust. It was a sinking feeling to realize that, under the circumstances, there was nobody. Jesus, I thought, how can there be nobody? There were three billion people in the world. Nobody?

One thing was sure: I couldn't sit in Barney's forever. For one thing, I didn't want those poor guys burning their eyes out staring at my knockers; and for another I had to get someplace where I could be alone and think.

"Can I get a taxi round here?" I asked the bartender.

"Where are you going?" one of the men asked.

"None of your business," I told him.

"There's Charley's Taxi," the bartender said.

"Charley's?" I asked, my voice thinning out for a moment; and then I realized there had to be more than one Charley in the world (though even one had become too many for my liking).

"He's all night," the bartender said. "You could call him."

"Do you know the number?" I asked.

He did. I got off of my stool and headed for the phone booth, my wiggling little backside being X-rayed by five pairs of eyes. I left the suitcase on the floor against the bar. I could see it from the phone booth and I thought the whole thing was very funny—leaving a half million dollars just sitting there, like it was so many jelly beans. And what was even funnier was those guys now whispering among themselves, about my boobs no doubt, with all that money no more than six feet away from them.

Charley's Taxi answered on the first ring.

"I'm at Barney's," I said, "and I need a ride."

"Where to?" he asked.

I hadn't thought of that. I paused. But then, where else? When things are really scrambled and screwed up, where else but the great big granddaddy of all that is scrambled and screwed up? Where else, really?

"New York," I said.

"New York City?" he asked.

"That's right."

He said, sounding apologetic, as if he was about to ruin my night, "That's thirty dollars, lady."

"How soon can you be here?" I asked.

I figured my luck was beginning to change when the guy who owned Charley's Taxi was not named Charley. His name was Rex, which is one hell of a name for anybody and especially so for a roly-poly, apple-cheeked cabbie wearing a chauffeur's cap.

"This is it," he said when we pulled away from Barney's. "Anybody else calls tonight is out of luck. My other cab's got a busted axle, so this is it."

I was barely listening. He'd invited me to sit in front with him—and I think he was being polite more than suggestive—but I chose to sit in the back. I was hoping he would take the hint and not become chatty—I had more than a little to think about. But there was no chance of that. He started in right away.

"What are you doing out here, lady?"

Shit, I thought. What was I going to tell this guy? It just wasn't in me to be impolite and tell him to shut up. In spite of my rather spotty record, I *did* have a good upbringing.

"I'm on my way home from college," I said.

"Which one?"

"Harvard."

"That's in Connecticut, isn't it?"

"I got lost."

He burst out laughing, taking off his chauffeur's cap and readjusting it on his head. He had fat little arms, like a baby's legs.

"You sure did," he said. "How'd you get so lost?"

"I don't know."

"You live in New York?"

And on and on. Every answer led to two more questions. He was sitting there with that cap on his head and a smile creased into his fleshy face, driving with one hand, his ball-of-fat elbow resting on the lowered window. He was really zipping along, the warm breeze racing back at me through the open window. I noticed he wasn't stopping for red lights or stop signs or anything; it was true there was no other traffic and I assumed he knew what he was doing. We always assume cab drivers know what they're doing, in spite of the dents in their fenders.

"You're lucky you didn't call me tomorrow night," Rex said. "That's when I drive Dr. Brody's wife home from her date. He thinks she goes to the movies, but she's got this guy out in the boondocks." He chuckled. "Meanwhile the doctor on Sundays is seeing Bentley's wife—he's the lawyer—who thinks she's playing tennis." He chuckled again. "These people screw around only with their own kind. I respect that. It sort of takes the curse off of it, don't you think? Huh?"

"Sure."

"But if it wasn't for me they couldn't do it, because they trust me, they know I don't talk."

"Why don't they take their own cars?" I asked.

"Wouldn't look good to be seen parked where they shouldn't be. They know what they're doing, these people. I could blow the town apart if I wanted, but I know how to keep shut. And they tip me real heavy. Nice people. What they do is their business. Don't you think?"

Yes, I thought, I do think, and would if you would only shut up.

Then he said, "Oh-oh." He was looking in his rear-view mirror. "State trooper," he said.

I turned around and there it was, a couple of hundred feet behind us, green dome light flashing round and round. It gave me a sinking feeling, since I figured it had to do with me. I don't know why I should have been scared of the cops, but I was. How do you explain two dead men and a half million dollars?

"Hold on, baby," Rex said, gunning the car. He hit the gas pedal and the cab fairly leaped ahead until the motor adjusted to the sudden acceleration.

I couldn't believe it. This clown was going to try to outrun the trooper. Now I really got scared. All of a sudden we were going through those dark roads and little nowhere towns at seventy miles an hour.

"What the hell are you doing?" I yelled, bouncing around in the back seat like a ball in a pinball machine.

"I passed a light back there," he said. He was driving with both hands on the wheel now, leaning forward, an expression on his face like a bulldog.

"You're crazy!" I said.

"Don't worry, lady; I know these roads like the back of my hand."

The trooper raised his siren now, a big whoop out of the night. I turned around again and there he was, really dogging us. Holy Christ, I thought, who the hell needed this?

"Stop the car!" I yelled. "Let me out!"

"Don't worry, lady," Rex yelled back. "Once I get across to New York State we'll be okay. I don't think they can touch you in another state."

He was taking turns on two wheels, going up and down little hills like a roller coaster. Twice in one night? I asked myself. How the hell many lives did I have? I saw myself going through the windshield like Big Stoney. With that vision in mind, I dropped onto the floor, hugging the suitcase. From down on the floor the damned car seemed to be going even faster. The siren kept blasting. I closed my eyes. Then we seemed to be floating for a second, I couldn't feel the road under me, and I squeezed my eyes shut and braced for the crash. But then we struck the road again, with a solid, jarring thump—Rex had gone over the crest of a hill at top speed, which I swear at the moment must have been ninety miles an hour.

"We're losing him!" he yelled.

"You son of a bitch!" I yelled back, so furious now I was crying.

"You okay, lady?" he asked with sudden concern. "Where the hell are you?"

"On the floor, you moron!" I shrieked.

"On the floor?"

"Keep your eyes on the fuckin' road!" I screamed, as loud as I could, figuring he was looking in the rear-view mirror for me. I think the profanity, coming from me, must have shocked him or something, because he didn't say anything after that.

He made a couple of fast turns that threw me against first one door and then the other. Then he went over an unpaved road that was bumpy as hell and I was shaken around like bunco dice. When we cleared that he made another sudden turn and then braked so hard I was thrown against the front seat. We had stopped. I couldn't believe it.

"Lost him," Rex said.

I looked up. His chubby face was peering down at me from over the top of the front seat, grinning under the visor of his cap.

"You okay?" he asked.

Shakily, I got to my feet, flopped back down in the seat, and drew a deep breath. We were parked in a narrow alley between two warehouses. I stared at him.

"Did you just ask me how I was?" I asked.

"Yeah," he said, nodding.

"Thank you. I feel fine," I said, feeling absolutely numb and breathless. "Where the hell are we?"

"On our way to New York," he said cheerfully, swinging around and arranging himself behind the wheel again. He turned the ignition. "Hey," he said, "no extra charge for the fun ride."

Chapter Eleven

Through no fault of his own, Rex delivered me alive and well at my destination. I paid him his thirty dollars and tossed in a twenty-dollar tip—not that he deserved it, but just to see how it felt to tip a twenty. It felt pretty damned good. Rex got very serious when he saw it coming, taking it with one hand and tipping his cap with the other.

I let him drop me off around the corner from my apartment. I had no intention of returning to it other than for a few minutes, to pick up some belongings. I wanted the ring my parents had given me when I graduated from high school, and my makeup kit, and my own goddamned toothbrush. It sounds crazy—that apartment was probably the most dangerous place in the world for me at the moment—but I was determined to go up there, to take the risk. I guess there was something psychological about it, too—you don't like to leave your home forever unless you know it's going to be forever. You want that one last goddamned look around. But even as I headed for it, believe me, I was appalled by the risk I was taking. In fact, I couldn't believe it. Christ, I was changing; I could feel it—changing by the minute. The sweet shock of near death must really be a wallop to the nervous system and everything else.

But I wasn't completely crazy. I stepped into a phone booth and dialed my number, just to make sure. It wouldn't be a good idea to walk in and find Charley sitting there, to see him look up and say, "Hey, you're supposed to be dead."

There was no answer. So I headed for the building, me and my suitcase. (I wasn't even thinking of what fun it was to be walking around the streets of New York late at night carrying a half million dollars in cash.) When I entered the lobby I asked the doorman if I had received any visitors. He said I hadn't. I took the elevator up to my apartment. I stood outside the door for about five minutes, listening. Satisfied no one was there, I let myself in.

I don't think the nightmare really hit me until I was inside and saw where I had been sitting, saw the book I had been reading, the cup of coffee I hadn't finished. It seemed like so long ago now, when life had been sweet and steady and untroubled. I wanted it all to come back, I wanted the last few hours not to have happened. It really hit me then, and I sat down and let it all out. I bawled like a baby, like ten babies, like a whole goddamned nursery. You can cry like nobody's business when you're alone. I must have sat for fifteen minutes, just crying and wailing and shaking, not trying in the least to hold it back, letting one wave after the other hit the beach.

What broke the spell was the telephone. All of a sudden it started to ring. I jumped up like from a hot stove and glared at the telephone as though it were a ticking bomb. It rang five times—I counted. I didn't draw a breath until it had stopped. Nobody ever called here except Charley, and since I was now supposed to be dead it meant that somebody else was expected here—either Mac and Big Stoney to wait for Charley, or maybe Charley himself.

I never moved so fast. I picked up the few things I had come for, stuffed them in with the money, had my last look around—why the hell that seemed so important I'll never know—and left.

Now I was good and scared. If somebody was coming there I might very well run into them in the lobby or out on the street. That sort of poor timing could be fatal. So I took the elevator down to the garage, figuring to leave from there. Boy, that was a spooky place—dimly lit, with rows of empty cars. I think next to cemeteries, public garages are the spookiest places. If I hadn't got murdered upstairs, I'd surely get mugged down there. Can you imagine some dumb-ass junkie mugging me and walking off with a half million?

When I walked up the ramp that led to the street I

found the big door closed. I didn't know how to open the damn thing, so I just stood there staring at it, as if trying to raise it by mental remote control. And then, all of a sudden, it started to go up in my face. The suddenness of it, the grumbling sound it made on the garage silence, scared the hell out of me, and I turned around and started to run—I guess I had been on the verge of panic anyway and this was all I needed to set it off. When I was halfway down the ramp a pair of bright headlights picked me up, and that shook me even more, even though I knew it was probably only some cluck coming home from the movies. God knows what *he* must have thought when he saw me running with my suitcase. But for all I knew it could have been Charley, coming to park there. The way things stood now, one slight miscalculation meant the ball game.

I ran into the garage, went through the exit door, and hurried up the stairs that led to the lobby. I walked through the lobby, said good night to the doorman, and went out into the street.

The first thing I did was hail a cab and jump in. I told the driver to cruise around until I made up my mind where to go. Again I thought of people, whirling names and faces through my mind. But, under these circumstances, there wasn't anybody. Just plain nobody.

I think I must have sat in that cab for an hour, cruising the midtown area. It wasn't just that I had nowhere to go: it was also the first relaxing moment I'd had in God knows when. I wanted to sit in the darkness—and the comfort and security—of that cab for as long as possible. The driver wasn't bothering me. He was a black man, wearing a baseball cap and smoking a cigar, and he seemed as uninterested in me as I was in him.

But I had to get out sometime and I finally directed him to a hotel on upper Madison Avenue, a pretty ritzy place. When we pulled up to the door I dug into my purse and came out with a hundred-dollar bill.

"I can't break it, lady," he said, pushing it back to me through the little two-way drawer in the divider.

"I don't want you to," I said. "Keep the change."

He stared at me, not in astonishment or gratitude, but

more like I was sick or something and he was sorry for me. Still staring at me, he took the bill, crumpled it up in his fist, and stuck it into an inside pocket of his jacket.

"Thank you," he said quietly.

When I got out he said to me through the window, "Good luck."

I watched him drive off. Then I went into the hotel. As I walked across the carpeting of this oh so quiet and dignified lobby, I could see the desk clerk sizing me up. I didn't like what I thought he was thinking. He was a tall, bony character with thin, neatly combed gray hair, a pink face, a cool eye, a little mouth with a pouting bottom lip; he was wearing a plaid jacket, a white-on-white shirt, and a bow tie. After everything that had happened, I was damned if I was going to take any crap from a guy who looked as though his fashion expert was a florist.

"I would like a room, please," I said looking him right in the eye. I must have still had the look of death, because he didn't give me any trouble, though I could tell he was suffering.

As I signed the register—using the name Tracy Fairbanks-Fletcher, which I thought was a good one for this place—I said, "Please have someone help me with my bag."

That must have convinced him I was truly class in spite of my casual appearance, because he pressed a button and a bellhop appeared. I wished I could have told the guy he was carrying a half million. Jeez, I thought, money could be a lot of fun, if people weren't such animals about it.

When I was alone in the room I closed the blinds and pulled the drapes and locked the door. Then I opened the suitcase and looked at the money again. It was prettier than color television. I must have sat and stared at it for about fifteen minutes, not with any big feelings of greed or possession or anything like that, but just staring at it and wondering about it. I think more than anything else at that moment I envied it, which is a peculiar way to think about money. But it was true, because here was something that had its own power, that was sought after and protected like nothing else in the world was.

When I was through daydreaming over the money I closed the suitcase and put it on the chair next to the bed. It was late now, well after midnight, but I wasn't tired or sleepy, nor was I hungry. It seemed almost pointless to eat or sleep; you needed those things in order to stay alive. But what did I have to stay alive for? It was just a matter of time before they caught up to me and finished the job. I was pretty much resigned to it. Especially since I had taken off with the money. That was going to piss them, positively. But I didn't regret having taken it; it was the only laugh I had on them. And I was going to enjoy it, too; tomorrow I was going to go out and buy myself the most expensive wardrobe—anything and everything I wanted, and price was no object.

The idea of spending that money lifted my spirits for a little while, but only a little while. Then they sank again, right through the soles of my shoes. That goddamned feeling of aloneness was building up again. It started nagging at me, all of a sudden, as if it hadn't been important before, and with it that infuriating question without an answer:

Why? Why?

And then I said, out loud, "Why not ask the son of a bitch?"

As I dialed the number of my apartment, I had these two feelings at once: anger and a sense of mischief. Boy, I thought, was he going to be surprised. If he was there.

He was.

Everything—the anger and the mischief—went away when I heard the sound of his voice—that gruff, impatient *Hello?* which carried weight and menace and authority and which said "If you're calling me it had damned well better be something important." He was there all right, my Charley, sitting in my apartment, thinking I was dead. The feeling I got was cold dread. Sure he sounded impatient; he was probably waiting to hear from his two charmers, wanting to know why they hadn't shown up yet with the money and the story of my demise.

"Hello?" he said again, his voice stronger. When Charley said hello to somebody he wanted them to say hello right back, and no two ways about it. You didn't answer Charley right away, you got a good crack in the face.

"Hello," I said flatly, trembling so much I was sitting on the bed holding on to the phone with both hands.

"Who is this?" he asked warily.

"Surprised to hear my voice, aren't you?" I said.

"Who is this?" he asked again. I believed he knew, but he wanted to hear it from me, to make sure.

"Terry," I said.

He paused. He was thinking. Man, was he thinking. I could see his face, his eyebrows coming together, his eyes narrowing, his lips bunching up—the way he always looked when he was considering some major problem.

"Where are you?" he asked, his voice quiet, cold. Well, give him credit for that—no false fun or friendship; Charley had too much pride to try and play the innocent.

"Never you mind," I said.

"Where are you?" he asked again.

"Why did you do it, Charley?" I asked, the emotion building up in my throat. "Jesus Christ, why the hell would you want to do that? What did I ever do to you? What did I do wrong?"

"Where are Mac and Stoney?"

"Never mind them. Answer me. Why? I have a right to know."

There was silence. He was thinking again, and probably about whether to play innocent or not. So positive was I that I was reading his mind correctly that I said, "Don't lie to me, Charley."

"Tell me where you are and I'll come over," he said.

"Oh, no. I don't want to see you again as long as I live." And then, like a real smart-ass, I added, sarcastically, "How long is that going to be, Charley?"

"You know I don't like to talk on the phone," he said. He was really burning, I could tell.

"Well, then I hope you don't mind listening. And I hope the goddamned phone is being tapped, because you tried to have me killed tonight, you lousy son of a bitch." I was crying now. "You want to know where your two gorillas are? Well, I can tell you. You can see them in Jersey, if you know what I mean. And I leave it to you to figure out how it happened. Don't hang up, Charley. There's more." The tears were streaming down my face now and I had to gulp a couple of times to catch my breath. "I've got the money. Figure that one out. I've got your lousy half million. How do you like that?"

"Bring it over here now," he said.

I gave him the horse laugh.

"I'll make you a deal," I said. "You tell me why you did it and I'll tell you where you can pick up the money."

He thought that one over. I knew he was thinking real hard, too, because Charley didn't like to have this kind of conversation over the telephone. The very fact that he was staying on so long showed how shook up he was, how serious this was for him.

"I didn't do anything," he said.

"Those bastards work for you."

"I didn't tell them to do anything."

"You're lying and I'm hanging up."

"Wait a minute," he said. Boy, were his wheels ever turning. "How can I tell you what I don't know?"

"You can tell me what you *do* know, and you don't have much time." I couldn't believe I was talking to him like that.

"You spoke to some cops," he said.

"They picked me up, Charley. I didn't tell them anything. How could I, when I don't *know* anything?"

He was unhappy about getting into this over the phone, but tough ships, Charley—he had no choice.

"It's not what *you* told *them*, it's what *they* told *you* ... about me. But I see now it was all a mistake, Terry. Come over here and I'll explain it all to you. Believe me, it was all a mistake, and I'm glad ..."

"Glad what?" I asked, my voice hard as nails.

"Glad it went wrong. Look, I don't care about the money; I just want to see you."

"Why?"

"Because it's been a while and I miss you," he said, trying to sound friendly and sincere, but he wasn't going to win any Academy Award for this one.

"How do I know I can trust you?"

"You know you can. I've just admitted it was all a mistake, haven't I?"

"Some mistake," I said with a flat little grunt.

"Look, talking over the phone like this isn't good for either one of us. Just get over here. Okay, baby?"

"You know what you can do, Charley?" I asked him.

"What?" he asked.

"Stand on your head and whistle Dixie through your asshole until I get there."

And I hung up.

So I had *that* much satisfaction anyway. Not that it had got me anywhere, except that I was feeling a peculiar sadness. Because I believed it now, the last shreds of doubt and disbelief had been peeled away: Charley had actually wanted me dead. God! Life's little surprises. But at least now I knew why. Because I had talked to the cops, despite the fact that I hadn't told them anything, because there was nothing I knew to tell. Didn't he understand that? (You don't have to ask yourself that one anymore, baby. No, he didn't understand.) And even if I *had* known something, didn't he realize he could trust me? (That's another one that doesn't need asking anymore, babes.) Or maybe it was just simply that I had been picked up and spun around in that car for a while; maybe it was like I was contaminated now.

But then I realized it wasn't that, that it was something more. Charley had said it; It wasn't what I had told the cops, but what *they* had told *me*. They had told me Charley's business. And they had done it on purpose—to make sure I knew, to make me feel implicated, and scared, and in trouble, so I would spill on him. Apparently they had been guessing that I knew something and could be scared into telling it. Oh, God, what a sloppy mess!

And another thing: How did Charley know so much about what went on between me and those cops? Either they wanted him to know, to scare *him* into making some kind of a move, or he had somebody on the inside. The latter, most likely. Him and his "Christmas" cops. He had plenty of people on the inside, like all those judges and politicos who were always so happy to shake his hand. Sons of bitches, what did they want from me? Christ, I couldn't even go to the *police* for protection. God knew which were his cops and which weren't.

It was getting awfully dark out.

Chapter Twelve

I woke up the next morning feeling gloomy as hell. I figured I was entitled. My only consolation was that Charley probably wasn't feeling much better. I was in the kind of situation where I slept all right; it was when I woke up that the nightmare started.

The first thing I saw when I opened my eyes was that suitcase standing on the carpet in the middle of the room, a little squared-around undistinguished-looking piece of baggage that contained a half million. That was worth staring at for at least ten minutes. All this propaganda about money that you hear—don't believe it. Here I was with a half million and what good was it going to do me? My life wasn't worth a plugged slug. Christ, this was a tough world to get some enjoyment out of.

I got out of bed, took a shower, and stepped out of it without drying myself. I'd always wanted to do that: drip-dry myself stark naked while walking around my living room, not worrying about the carpet getting wet. Only it wasn't a living room but a fancy hotel room uptown on Madison. I pulled the drapes, opened the blinds, lifted the window, and felt New York's balmy breezes on my naked belly. That was another new experience: standing bare-assed at the window. Doing all those silly things I'd always wanted to do, because I knew at any moment I could be blown into oblivion by an ice-cold trigger finger. I wasn't being an exhibitionist, I didn't care if anybody saw me or not. In fact, the only one who took notice of me was an old woman in the building across the street who was cleaning the windows. She glanced once and that was all.

Then I had the fiendish idea to spill all the money out of the window onto Madison Avenue, just for the hell of it, to see what would happen. Boy, what a circus that would be! That idea, though, was a bit *too* looney. I was going to need that money, if I was going to get any joy and satisfaction out of my last days on earth.

It's strange how you can suddenly start thinking of death in such a matter-of-fact way, accepting it without fear. Maybe the experience I'd had the night before, coming so close to it, was influencing my thinking now. Why wasn't I afraid now? Well, thinking about it, it seemed to me that what had made last night so scary was the fact that it was being suddenly thrust upon me without warning and by someone else's decision, without any reason or logic whatever, as far as I could tell. But now it was different. I was expecting it, and when you expect something to happen you're contributing to making it happen to a certain extent. So it was like I was part of the decision now. I know this sounds crazy and half-baked, but that was how I felt. Hell, I wasn't happy about it, but at least I wasn't going into hysterics over it.

I got dressed and then phoned for room service. After I ate I sat around watching television. At noon I called room service again, for lunch this time. After I'd eaten a lonely, boring lunch I began to realize what was going on—I was afraid to leave the room. After all the big mental heroics about expecting death and not being afraid, there I was, sitting in that goddamned room like a hermit. Jesus Christ, I suddenly thought, at forty dollars a day, worked out to around twelve hundred a month, or fourteen thousand a year, I could sit in that room for about thirty years if I wanted with the money I had. Thirty years ought to be enough time for things to cool down.

Better to die in the sunlight than to live in the shadows, I told myself (which is about as philosophical as I get), and then went out. I stuffed five thousand into my handbag and headed for the Fifth Avenue shops to outfit myself. The only clothes I had were what I was wearing on my back.

I had myself a glorious afternoon. Spent two thousand dollars on a new wardrobe and shoes. Then I went to a beauty parlor and had my hair dyed blond and restyled. I wasn't too crazy about the way I looked, but I did look somewhat different.

The new look gave me some confidence and I started going out every afternoon, just walking on Fifth Avenue, or going through Central Park and feeding the pigeons. I tried not to look too glamorous on these outings, wearing print dresses and flats and a babushka on my head. The hotel was no doubt beginning to think me some sort of eccentric. After a week the assistant manager stopped me in the lobby and very apologetically told me it was the hotel's policy to settle "each suite's obligation at least once a week." I'm sure it was a new rule they'd put in just for me.

"How much do I owe you?" I asked.

"Three hundred twenty-five dollars," he said.

I opened my bag, took out four hundred, gave it to him, and told him to keep the change. That took care of *him*.

I was aching to call my parents, but there were too many reasons not to. For one thing, I didn't want to get them at all involved. For all I knew, Charley was having their goddamned phone tapped. Another thing was, it wouldn't have done any good. They'd written me off a long time ago, and to suddenly call and tell them I was in trouble would only have earned me a lot of I-told-you-so's. There wasn't a thing they could do for me. But there was something I could do for them. I took a packet of hundreds—ten thousand dollars' worth—put it in a manila envelope, and mailed it to them, anonymously. I would have sent them more but I was afraid too much money would only scramble their brains and do more harm than good.

I tried to imagine the scene as my mother lumbered downstairs to get the morning mail, brought up that envelope, opened it, and saw ten thousand dollars tumble out. What would they do with it? God knows. My father liked to invest on the ponies, I knew that; but my mother knew it too. It wouldn't have surprised me in the least if she just took that windfall and tucked it into the mattress without telling anybody. Good old Mom. Careful, careful, careful. Direct opposite of daughter Terry.

Then, after about two weeks, something else began to happen. I was getting lonely, and horny. I'd barely spoken to a soul the whole two weeks. I was living a lifestyle alien to my natural self. I enjoyed people, enjoyed male companionship, and I was beginning to miss those things. I thought it would be nice to go out and pump some excitement into my life.

Maybe I was feeling overconfident. What the hell—two weeks had gone by and I was still alive. Indestructible Terry. Charley might be forgetting about me, figuring I'd taken off to Rio or Paris or someplace with his swag. Hell, he had plenty of other things to think about besides me. And anyway, he wouldn't be looking for me in New York—that's the last place I'd be, right?

So I dolled myself up in a pair of tight-assed pants, a tight blouse that V-necked somewhere down between daring and scandalous, a lightweight topcoat, high heels, and went out on the town.

I suspected the East Side and Broadway areas could mean trouble, if anyplace could, so I took a cab down to Greenwich Village. I very seldom ever went there, because Charley had never liked it. The oddball characters turned him off. For all his badness, Charley could be very square about certain things. He didn't like hippies or fags or anybody who was personally peculiar, nor did he like to see racially mixed couples.

I wasn't particularly fond of the Village myself, but when I got down there I must admit I felt kind of comfortable. With all of those oddies walking around nobody paid too much attention to me—I was lost in the crowd and it felt good.

After walking around aimlessly for a half hour or so, I stepped into a bar. It was one of those places that put great emphasis on "atmosphere"—it was practically midnight in there, with the only illumination coming from the back-bar lights and from glass-enclosed candles on the tables. There was a crowd at the bar, though the place wasn't jammed. There was a nice at-home feeling at being close to people and smoke and laughter again.

I edged up to the bar, wondering how long it would

take for some bundle of nerve and sexual energy to step forth and begin operating. I'd say it took all of four minutes from the time I walked in.

"I *am* going to buy you a drink, aren't I?" he said.

He was standing behind me, with long blond hair down to his shoulders and a neatly trimmed Van Dyke. He was a big guy, with good shoulders and biceps in a short-sleeved polo shirt with horizontal pinstripes. Not a bad specimen, I thought. Not bad at all. And very sure of himself.

"I guess you are," I said.

"Naturally I am," he said. "I knew that the moment you walked in. I believe, in a limited way, in destiny."

"You're destined to buy me a drink, are you?" I asked.

"It was written in the book of life ten thousand years ago that we would meet here tonight and that I would buy you a drink," he said.

Boy, Greenwich Village bullshit. There was nothing like it anywhere. I remembered it from my premistress, premurder target days when I used to come down here in my Bronx overcoat, Bronx hair-do, Bronx earrings, and Bronx virginity, and thrill to it all—when I thought all these guys were starving artists or tubercular poets (most of them turned out to be Seventh Avenue Herbies taking a night off from the Belles of Forest Hills).

"Listen," I said, "how long are we destined to stand here talking about destiny?"

He shouldered past me up to the bar and signaled the bartender with a thumb-and-forefinger circle.

"What are you drinking?" he asked me.

"Bourbon on the rocks."

"Twin bourbons on the rocks," he told the bartender. Then he asked me my name.

"Alexandra," I said. I always liked that name. "What's yours?"

"Felix," he said. I almost started to laugh but saw he was serious about it. A big handsome hunk like that named Felix. But what's in a name?

"You from out of town?" he asked.

"Cleveland," I said.

"That's considered out of town," he said. "San Francisco is not, Boston is not. But Cleveland is. So is Philadelphia and Los Angeles."

"Who decides?" I asked.

"I do."

The drinks came. He pulled a fiver from his blue jeans and put it on the bar.

"How about you?" I asked.

"How about me?" he said.

"Where are you from?"

"Maine, originally. Right now I'm a New Yorker."

"What do you do for a living?" I asked. All the great old questions we used to ask guys at dances. Next I'd want to know if he had a car, then if he could do the frug.

"I haven't decided yet," he said. "What else do you want to know?"

"That's it," I said.

We put away a few more bourbons while he jabbered on about life in Greenwich Village. I guess he really believed I was from Cleveland. He didn't seem at all curious about me—about where I lived, what I did, or any of those solid middle-class things.

"What made you come in here?" he asked.

"Destiny," I said.

"You a thrill-seeker?"

"It depends."

"You had a lot of them lately?" he asked.

"What?"

"Thrills."

"You don't know the half of it."

"People in Maine," he said, "don't believe what it's like down here. Last time I was home my grandfather started asking me about the Village. He's never been off his potato patch his whole life. Wanted some vicarious thrills, I guess. Asked me about all the strange people. Wanted to know what a dyke was."

"You tell him?" I asked.

"Sure. Vividly. He's old enough to know. I told him just what a dyke was. He was impressed. Then my father comes home from work—he's a foreman in a factory up there—and starts telling us what a hell of a day he had on the job. One thing after another going wrong. Soon as he solved one problem, another popped up. 'I had my finger in the dike all day long,' he said. You should have seen the old man perk up. 'You had your finger *where* all day?' "

Felix gave a big hearty Viking laugh. I didn't believe a word of it, but I laughed anyway.

I'd had about four drinks and was starting to feel woozy. That close atmosphere was beginning to tell. The place was getting smaller. Felix had his big arm around me, his fingers firmly on my flat little tummy. Then he leaned his beard close to my face and I thought he was going to kiss me, but instead he said, "Well, shall we?"

"Shall we what?" I asked. Innocent little Alexandra from Cleveland.

"Repair to my place," he said.

"Where is that?"

"Two short blocks thither."

He was staring me dead in the eye.

"What did you have in mind?" I asked.

"Sex," he said, then gave me a slow smile in that beard. He had a tooth missing in front, which I hadn't noticed before.

"How'd you lose that tooth?" I asked.

"Defending a woman's honor," he said.

"Now you want to get even, do you?"

"I'll tell you, Alexandra," he said, "in this uncertain nuclear age people should grab what simple, natural pleasures are available without undue procrastination." His voice was solemn, but there was a cute little twinkle in his eye.

"I've never gone to bed with anybody named Felix," I said.

"Is that because of a prejudice," he asked, "or is it simply bad luck?"

"I don't know."

"It's a fine old Roman name. There were some very distinguished gentlemen of ancient Rome named Felix."

"You look more like a Viking," I said.

Now he pulled me against him and I could feel his Viking hammer jammed between my legs. The twinkle was gone from his eye, replaced by a look of strong determination. I knew that look. Men got very serious about sex during those moments just before the final decision was made. I don't know whether they were trying to show their virility or their need or what. It was just the opposite of the look you got when it was all over, when they rolled their heads on the pillow, sized you up with an expression almost of annoyance, as if to say, "Christ, are *you* still here?"

"Show me the way, Felix," I said.

After we'd left the place, I had to go back and retrieve my bag, which I'd left on the bar. I had to laugh at my cool absentmindedness: I had about five or six grand stuffed in that bag. That was my usual walking-around money in those days. You never knew when you might want to take a cab or buy an ice cream cone, right?

Felix gathered me to him with a strong, possessive arm as we moved through the crowd flow. Inside of half a block I smelled incense, mustard, pot, a fart, and one or two other aromas that I couldn't identify; I heard at least three different languages and saw a drunk lying in his own puke in a doorway, a couple holding ice cream cones aloft and kissing, a teenager with tears in her eyes, and a policeman yawning.

We walked two blocks to a brownstone walk-up on East Eleventh Street. Felix had been pretty quiet until we got to his building. Then he said, "I think we're being followed."

I turned around in a hurry; the street was dark and empty.

"I don't see anybody," I said.

He turned around. "They were there a moment ago."

"Who was there?" I asked.

"Two men."

"What makes you think they were following us?" I asked.

"We were walking east on Eighth and they were walking west. Then we were all walking east."

"What did they look like?" I asked. We were standing in

front of his building, at the foot of the tall flight of steps that led to a dimly lit vestibule.

He shrugged. "Two guys," he said. "Who cares? They're gone now."

"Then maybe they weren't following us," I said.

"I was probably mistaken. Forget it."

I was peering into the darkness.

"You worried about something?" he asked.

"I don't like being followed," I said.

"Don't fret, baby, you're just a natural-born leader," he said and kissed me softly on the ear. That message got through in a hurry.

"Let's go upstairs," I said.

It was two flights up, on stairs whose creaks were muffled under ratty-looking carpeting. The light bulbs must've been 20-watters, that hallway was so goddamned dim; the shadows were flung along the walls like half-finished paint jobs.

He had three small rooms, furnished bachelor-style. The kitchen had linoleum on the floor—Christ, I hadn't seen that in years—and looked like it was never used. The living room had a crummy-looking sofa and a couple of soft chairs—the kind that wheezy grandfathers like to sit in. A rug covered most of the floor. I didn't have to ask to know that this place came furnished. The view was across a courtyard to the windows of a factory, which was dark now.

The bedroom was the action center of this layout. The bed looked like it hadn't been made in years (though I guessed that a lot of women had been made in it); either it was a sex nest or else the guy who slept in it had a lot of nightmares. My money was on the nest.

He turned on a lamp that stood on a bureau. That bulb couldn't have been more than 20 watts either; Christ, wasn't this building properly wired? Then he pulled off his polo shirt and dropped it onto the foot of the bed. He had a physique, this guy, like a heavyweight boxer. He knew it, too. They always do, these muscle guys. You can see the conceit in the way they carry themselves—shoulders high and rigid, chest out. Then he started unbuckling.

"Hey," I said.

He stopped, looking at me.

"No preliminaries?" I asked.

"What would you like?"

"Poetry," I said, feeling snotty.

"June–moon," he said.

"That's not so hot."

"How about hick–prick?" he said. "I am, after all, from a small town in Maine."

"That's pretty," I said. "Do you know any more?"

"Fuck–suck."

"Hot shit."

"Doesn't rhyme," he said.

"Screw–you?"

"Depends on how you're saying it."

"This is terribly romantic," I said.

"Penis, Venus?"

"I like that."

We were standing on opposite sides of the bed. He dropped his hand to his crotch.

"You aiming that thing at me?" I asked.

"Erection correction," he said.

"I thought maybe you were a pecker-checker," I said. Boy, I thought that was clever. Proud of myself, I was.

"Now let's have some tit-wit," he said.

I answered that one by opening my blouse, sliding it off, and letting it drop to the floor. Hell, I had just as good a physique as he did, gender for gender, and was just as proud. My boobs hung out firm and hard in what I once saw described as their "nylon cradles." He let go of his crotch and ran the back of his hand across his beard.

"Where'd you develop that chest?" he asked.

"You drink a lot of milk and then bend over," I said. "What about yours?"

He shrugged. "Fucking is hard work."

Now he unbuckled his jeans and dropped them to the floor and stepped out of them. He wasn't wearing any underwear, this guy—I'd never known a man to do that before. And I was right, that thing *was* aiming at me, a big old hammer, swollen to the ready, pointing at me like an M-1 out of the bushes.

"Is it always like that?" I asked.

"Unlike the average man," he said, "my prick is a muscle and my heart a prick."

Now I unhooked my bra and swung it around for a moment like a hooker with her handbag and let it fly away.

"I don't know why you wear that thing," he said. "They haven't budged an inch."

Then he got onto the bed and came across to me, pulled me down with one hand, and unbuttoned my pants. Gently, he slipped them down, studying with narrowed eyes what he was unveiling. When the pants were gone he leaned forward and took a handful of hot, anxious snatch and caressed. I had an intake of breath and closed my eyes. The next thing I knew my bikini panties were gone—with a rip. I mean, he tore them right off. I opened my eyes.

"What have you got against underwear?" I asked.

"I don't like to have anything against underwear," he said, getting on top of me with that Maine lumberjack–heavyweight champ body. I smelled the bourbon through his beard as he came forward and gave me a long, wet, suckling, scratchy kiss. I put my hands on his biceps and squeezed, feeling the strength packed in there.

He came into me like an invasion, filling me up. He was a considerate lover, displaying fine control and staying with it until he had brought me off. When finally he did come it was with growling satisfaction and intensity, and then he got rough, pounding against me vigorously until he'd blasted himself dry right down to the dregs.

Then he rolled over to one side with a big sigh, like he was deflating—no staying in and "soaking his pickle," as the boys in the Bronx used to say—and lay there panting, gazing up at the ceiling. Looking at him sideways, his eyes looked white and shiny.

"I'm lucky," he said. "Lucky, lucky."

"Why?" I asked.

"It always feels like the first time. No matter how many times I do it, every day, every night, five times a night—

it's always like the first time. Did I communicate that to you?"

"Yes," I said, which was a lie; I hadn't been thinking about him at all. I'd been so pent up inside from inactivity that I'd felt like a rocket going off and I swear if that throbbing hulk of muscular passion hadn't been on top of me there would have been a lift-off.

After several minutes during which we just lay there next to each other, not saying anything, not even touching, he said, "Isn't it odd? After two strangers have sex they find they have nothing to say to one another."

"I'll think of something soon," I said. I was feeling too good to talk; talking can sometimes spoil a nice feeling. I hadn't simmered down yet; some odds and ends were still flying around inside.

"Want something to drink?" he asked.

"You have wine?"

"No."

"I'm in the mood for wine," I said.

"I've got a bottle of something in the kitchen."

"A bottle of what?"

"Something," he said. "I don't know what; I seldom go into my kitchen."

I got the feeling that he was a sponger. A lot of these big, good-looking sexual steam shovels are. It's no problem for them to find adoring women who'll feed them and bed them and probably help with a few bucks now and then. But, hell, I wasn't going to criticize him for it if he was, not after the lifestyle I'd been following these past few years. If you've got brains, you use them; if you've got a body, you use *it*. It's a tough world to get by in. Some people lie and wheedle their way through life, others smile their way, some cheat, some outsmart. You examine the arsenal nature gave you and pick out the weapons you can best use. Everybody's got a talent or an ability or a fault. Yeah, even faults. If you're a doormat you can get along too, by permitting people to step on you, since a lot of people love to step on others. A doormat person can always get a job and have friends.

Felix got up.

"I'll see what's there," he said.

I watched that big naked body go through the doorway into the unlighted living room. A moment later the kitchen light went on. Christ, I hadn't noticed it before, but his bed stank. The sheets looked like they hadn't been changed in years; they had such a soft, wrinkliness to them, like they'd been just about worn through, which didn't surprise me, not the way this guy went at it. I wondered how many other women he'd love-hammered on these sheets before me. Maybe as many as five hundred? What a depressing thought.

"Felix," I called out.

"What?" he asked from the kitchen.

"How many women have you laid in this bed?"

"Just two," he said. "You and my grandmother."

Big shot. Wanted me to think there had been thousands.

"I believe you," I said, and laughed. Then that laugh froze in my throat and a silly little smile froze on my lips and I sat up, resting on my hands. I'd left my handbag on that crummy little chest of drawers he had near the doorway and now it wasn't there. I got up on my knees and crawled over to the edge of the bed and looked down at the floor. It wasn't there either. I looked under the bed, then all around the room, under my clothes, his clothes. That son of a bitch! I had thousands of bucks in there!

I went through the dark living room and walked into the light that fell from the kitchen. There he was, big bare ass toward me, going through the handbag on the kitchen table.

"You bastard," I said.

He whirled around. He didn't like being caught—his eyes told me that; they looked mean, then quickly turned curious. The curiosity was just as mean. Never before have I been that naked and had somebody looking only into my eyes.

"You counted it yet?" I asked.

"No," he said.

"I'll save you the trouble. There's between five and six thousand."

"I'll be goddamned," he said. This big gorilla didn't like

being surprised. He was a wise-ass and a cynic with a big ho-hum for the world, and now he'd been taken completely by surprise. Thought he'd known it all, seen it all, heard it all.

"I cleaned out my bank account this morning," I told him. "I'm going to Australia tomorrow."

"Sure you are," he said.

"You've got a hell of a nerve, sweetie," I said. "Is this how you make a living? I would have given you twenty if you'd asked for it. You were worth it."

"You a hooker?" he asked.

That was pretty naïve for a man of the world. A hooker with that kind of dough?

"That's right," I said. "You want to make your donation now?"

He pointed his finger at me.

"You're no hooker," he said. Then he looked at my arms, looking for tracks. None there. Many things, old chum, but never, never that. He frowned, this stark-naked giant standing there holding my little old handbag. I'll tell you one thing—don't ever underestimate the lure and seduction of money: his enormous joystick had shrunk down to the size of a thumb—and that's with Terry Terrific standing there before him with all secrets bared.

"You're a pusher," he said.

"Uh-uh."

"Then what? Some mixed-up rich kid? A bank robber? What?"

"None of your business."

"This is driving me crazy," he said, raising the bag and shaking it.

"Then you ought to hand it over and forget about it," I said.

He gave me a blank look. He was going to have to do some heavy thinking now. Give it back? All that dough? Christ, I could just see his guts churning. Hell, I didn't need the money. It was a drop in the bucket. With the right sob story, like his little old Ma needing an operation or something, I would have *given* it all to him. But there was a principle involved now. The son of a bitch had been trying to *rob* me.

I can tell you what my instincts were: Get the hell out of there. Tell him to stick the bankroll up his ass and get out. But I was full of righteous indignation, unfortunately. You get the feeling that if you back down you'll be in mourning for your conscience for the rest of your life. If you have a rest of your life.

I didn't know how mean this guy could be. You never can tell. Here he had been probably expecting to filch a ten from me and instead had stumbled into Fort Knox. That kind of money could turn a guy from petty to desperate and dangerous in a hurry. How badly had he wanted the ten? That was the question now, because whatever had been driving him in the first place was now multiplied by at least five hundred.

It would have been ironic as hell, after surviving my ride with two of Charley's top torpedos, to have some creep Viking stud wring my neck in this dump, cut me up, and lower me down the dumbwaiter bone by bone.

"I could take all of it," he said, "and you couldn't do a thing about it."

"If you mean I couldn't out-wrestle you for it, you're right," I said. "But I could go to the police."

"No," he said, shaking his head. "Never. Obviously, this is tainted loot. It can't be otherwise. You have no legitimate business having it, so there's no way you'd ever go to the police about its loss. Am I right?"

He was right, the son of a bitch; but I didn't let him know it, not with a blink or a budge, I didn't; I just continued staring right at him, cold as ice.

"Aren't you afraid somebody might come visit you?" I asked.

"So you're a mob girl, are you?" he said.

"I never said that."

"You're implying."

He took a fistful of bills from the bag and squeezed them in his fist. He'd gotten attached to that dough. After staring at it for about a half-minute, he looked at me, a playful little smile in his beard. He'd made a decision.

"I'm keeping it," he said softly.

"Do you think that's right, Felix?" I asked.

"I'm keeping it," he said, his voice flat and hard now. That decision was now chiseled into stone.

I turned around and went back to the bedroom. I didn't know what the hell I was going to do, but whatever it was, I wanted to be dressed when I did it. I guess he was more puzzled than curious, because he didn't follow. Hurriedly, I hooked on my bra, looked at my torn-apart panties, then picked up my pants and blouse and put them on. Then I put on my shoes. I went back into the kitchen. He smiled when he saw me.

"I hate to see you leave, Alexandra," he said. "I really do."

"What are you going to do with my money?" I asked.

"Whose money?" he asked. "Money has no true or permanent owner. A few minutes ago it was yours, now it's mine."

"A kid like you can get into a lot of trouble with that much money," I said, sounding like a big-shot lady of the world. That much money. I had to laugh to myself. That, literally, was walking-around money.

"It won't be spent foolishly or unwisely," he said. "I'm going to use it for my redemption and salvation. I don't belong in a dump like this. You'll agree with that, won't you?"

He put the bag down on the table and faced me with crossed arms, grinning at me. I was good and sore now, but wasn't showing it. Always the lady.

"Listen," I said, "the least you can do is give me back my ID cards and five bucks for cab fare."

He nodded. "My pleasure," he said.

He uncrossed his arms and turned for the bag, and that's when I went at him. I don't know if I'd been planning it; all I know was that all of a sudden I had to do something and now was the chance. I ran into him full force with my shoulder and knocked him backwards. I guess I must have caught him off balance because he really went, taking the table with him. His legs flew up as he went, his balls and pecker rattling, and then he crashed over in front of the stove, wedged by the overturned table, stunned for a moment, his eyes rolling and storming with surprised anger. I picked up the handbag and ran out the door, yelling, "Fuck you, Felix!"

Chapter Thirteen

I ran down those stairs as fast as I could. I never thought he'd follow; what the hell, he was naked. But money—again, never underestimate its drawing power. I had reached the first landing when I heard him. I took one look, saw that big old pecker bouncing and flapping, and ran like hell, screaming for help. But not a door opened; in fact, running past one I heard a bolt slide into place. New Yorkers. Live and let die. Never get involved.

When I reached the street door he wasn't far behind. I threw it open and went clattering down the front stoop. Ever try running in high heels? When I hit the sidewalk I looked back. Surely he wouldn't come after me now, stark naked, into the street. But, Jesus Christ, there he was, like some fricking goddamned caveman who'd just had his ass toasted by a burning stone, throwing aside the door and bursting right out into good old New York City, wearing nothing more than his beard and a murderous expression. Good God, I thought, I'm about to be done in on the sidewalk by a naked lunatic.

I started running. The son of a bitch would be on me in a few seconds. I had the bright idea to start scattering the money around—that would stop him. It was a good idea, but my brain was too chaotic at the moment to communicate the message to my hands, and I didn't do anything but run, in my high heels.

Then I saw the guy there. He seemed to just be standing there, in front of a store that had black shades rolled down its windows.

"Help!" I yelled, figuring that would surely make him disappear. It takes guts to help a stranger in the night, and double guts when the stranger is being pursued by a naked man. But I'll be damned if he didn't move, right into the line of fire. He stepped out after I'd passed him and got between me and Felix. I heard them collide and I stopped running. Hell, the guy was trying to help me; I couldn't let him do it all by himself, especially when he was about a head shorter than Felix the Ox.

When I turned around they had wrestled off of the sidewalk into the street and Felix was yelling at him. Then the guy hit him and Felix stumbled back.

"You bastard!" Felix yelled and charged the guy.

Pity the poor stranger, I thought. I took off one of my high heels and ran up to help, gripping the shoe like a hammer. I'd heard that one of those heels could do real damage if you swung it right, and I had every intention of swinging it right; no poor stranger was going to get punched away on my account if I could help it. But I was underestimating the stranger. Holy shit, I thought, I had lucked into the heavyweight champ. The guy was doing a job on huge Felix that was unbelievable. He sent a right and a left into Felix's belly that doubled the big bastard in two, then finished him off not with fists but by bringing his knee up into Felix's chin, a shot that knocked the big guy flying and left him flat in the street.

"God bless you, mister!" I yelled, limping up to him on my one shoe. I was about to throw my arms around him and kiss him; in fact I had my two arms up and ready for the embrace when he turned around, a slow, mean smile on his face.

"Why, thank you, Terry," he said softly.

That imperfect little computer that is my brain did a whirl or two: we had been followed from the bar. Oh, God, I thought, they were two of Charley's boys. They'd picked me up on the street and followed and waited.

I dropped my arms and backed away.

"Leave me alone," I said.

He was walking toward me, a powerful-looking son of a bitch in a black fedora and black raincoat. If he'd made hamburger out of big Felix without so much as missing a breath, what was he going to do to me? I turned around and saw a car moving slowly along the street. There was the other one.

123

"I've got a gun!" I yelled, fumbling in my handbag for a second. That gave him pause for a moment and I threw my shoe at him, then turned and ran across the street toward the only sign of life on that street—an all-night garage. Running on my one shoe like a cripple I ran into the garage. An attendant was sitting in the office watching television and he never even looked up.

There was a ramp that wound up into utter darkness, and I followed it. I paused for just a moment to kick off my other shoe, then kept going. The ramp wound up past one level of cars to another. I was halfway up to the second level when I saw the headlights flash on the wall from below and heard the car roaring up. They were really moving, too; I heard tires screeching as they made the turn, a real hysterical sound.

I was gasping and sobbing, wondering where the hell I was going. The second level was it. There wasn't any more. I looked back down the ramp—that was the only way in or out, and it was filled with big bright headlights.

There weren't many cars up there, just a few, and they were spaced far apart. The place was wide open. I didn't see any doors, nothing but big ugly blank walls, except for one side that faced out on the street and was open air, with nothing there but an iron railing. I ran across the concrete to the railing and looked out. There was nothing but dark buildings, and in the street nobody but naked Felix lying in sweet slumber. Suddenly the headlights swept over me. I was too scared to move. And anyway, where the hell was I going to go?

I just stood there, pressing my back against the iron railing. The headlights were bearing down on me, getting further and further apart, and I realized the car was accelerating. They had me dead to rights and were going to finish the job with grillwork. I could practically feel that goddamned car smashing into my belly and oozing me through that iron railing like something coming out of a meat grinder.

I could see them behind the windshield, two son-of-a-bitchin' ghouls about to send my guts up through my mouth. I was too dumbstruck even to scream. And then I was moving, but I swear my legs were acting on their own, because my brain was frozen, numb, dead. I didn't run or dart: I dove. I went through the air sideways and hit the cold, hard, grease-smelling concrete just as the car flew by.

There was a little curb there and the car hit it and bounced up violently. Lying on the ground, twisted around, I watched it go right on crashing through that iron railing, which suddenly flew apart like an opening gate and the car still going, right out into thin air. I twisted around again and watched it go. For a moment it looked like it might sail right onto the rooftop across the street; it was in mid-air, straight out, its wheels spinning. Then it began to drop, the hood pointed slightly forward. It dropped into the street with an awful crash, seemed to sink for a moment as it hit, but then, like something that had been gathering and coiling its strength it suddenly bounced into the air and shot forward, jumping the curb, and plowing through that window with the black shades. There was a terrific roar and crash of breaking glass as the car buried its snout in the store.

The view was terrific, but those bastards might have survived the occasion, so I got up and ran back down the winding ramp. When I got to the street the garage attendant was outside, walking cautiously toward the mess. He gave me a startled look. Boy, was he going to have a tale to tell: a car drops out of the sky, a naked guy is lying in the street (that car didn't miss old Felix by much), and then this piece of ass comes running by without shoes.

I kept running, out to where there were lights and cars and people. Then I stopped, caught my breath, and tried to compose myself. I spotted a cab waiting at a red light and hurried over and got in.

"Where to, lady?" the driver asked.

"Give me a minute to think it over," I said.

Chapter Fourteen

It took more than a minute to think it over. *Where to, lady?* Good question, buddy. Any suggestions? It didn't seem to make any difference where; every place seemed about the same, since none of them had very much future. What scared and depressed me more than anything else was the fact that Charley still had his goons out looking for me and that they had spotted me, out of eight million. Those two cuddlebugs had no doubt been combing the city for me and just by luck had picked me out in the Village. Well, it was my own fault for going there.

So where, then? I mean, after I went back to the hotel, picked up my money and whatever I could squeeze into a suitcase, and checked out. Where to then? Christ, I didn't have the foggiest. Miami? Vegas? Acapulco? Those were the only kinds of places I knew. But they were Charley's places. How long would I last in any of them? Shit. After a couple of weeks of my confidence gradually building up, it was all gone again. *Poof,* like that. They had spotted me in the crowds, even with my phony blond hair. And I don't think those bastards even knew me—they'd probably been studying pictures of me.

The cabbie broke into my thinking with a quaint suggestion.

"Hey, lady," he said as we paused at a red light.

"What?"

"If you go down on me I'll forget the fare."

"Listen, you son of a bitch," I said, "how would you like to be reported to the hack bureau?"

"Go ahead," he said. "Tell 'em anything you want. I'll deny it. It's your word against mine. I'll tell them you propositioned me. They'll take my word on it, believe me. They know what kinds of creeps we pick up at night."

He was very calm about it. All in the ordinary, everyday flow of conversation. Nice weather. Heavy traffic. How'd the Mets do? How about a blow job? And other chitchat.

The light changed and we started up again, cruising across Thirty-fourth Street. He was a beefy guy with a head as bald as a bowling ball. Around forty or forty-five; you can't always tell with baldies. I looked at his ID card and photo. Big round smiling face. Conrad Plicker. Just what I needed in my life at the moment: a Conrad Plicker.

"What do you say?" he said.

"I say go to hell."

"The fare's gonna be near four dollars."

"I can stand it," I said.

"I hope I didn't insult you," he said.

"No, you didn't insult me," I said. "People are always asking me to do them favors."

He shrugged.

"I figured I'd try," he said. "You can't blame a guy for trying."

"What's the matter with you, don't you need the money?" I asked. I was so nervous and upset I was glad for conversation—any conversation, even a discussion about blow jobs with Conrad Plicker.

"Don't worry about me," he said.

"Four dollars can buy a lot of milk for your kids."

"That's true."

"How many kids you got?"

"Five," he said holding up the fingers of one hand.

"Don't you love your wife?"

"What's that got to do with it?" he asked.

"You'd be betraying her," I said. Shit on him, I thought. Shit on his wife, too, and his five kids.

"Don't get personal, lady."

"Look who's talking about getting personal."

"I'm sorry if I insulted you," he said.

"Do you proposition all the women who get into your cab?"

"Only the pretty ones," he said with a little laugh. Cool Conrad Plicker.

"Well, I don't see how you can afford to give up four dollars, what with five kids to support."

"I guess you're right. Just trying to do you a favor, that's all."

"I can afford the fare," I said.

"Okay then."

"I'm not as poor as I look."

"I never said you looked poor. In fact, you look kind of ritzy."

"Thanks," I said.

"And built like a destroyer."

"Thanks again."

"What the hell," he said.

When we pulled up to the hotel I fished a fifty out of my bag, got out, and handed it to him through the window.

"Keep the change," I told him, then leaned through the window, put my hand on his bald head, and kissed him right on top of it. I was wearing sticky red lipstick and left a pair of lips imprinted on him. Let him explain *that* to his wife and five kids. Then in my best throaty, seductive voice I whispered, "You're my kind of man, Conrad." Then I walked away.

"Hey, lady," he said.

I turned around. He was sitting there holding the fifty, an absolutely dumbfounded look on his face.

"You're not wearing any shoes," he said.

"No shit," I said.

I hurried into the hotel and crossed the lobby to the elevator. The bowl-of-fruit desk clerk was watching me; I could feel him watching me. He was no doubt wondering what this crazy broad was doing now, walking through the lobby of this overpriced pile of snobbery without any shoes. He should know that I had also just been chased down the street by a naked gorilla who'd tried to rob me, been almost murdered by two friends of a friend, and propositioned in a taxi cab. The elevator was slow in coming, so I turned around and frowned at the clerk, just in time to see him lower his head. Never allow yourself to be caught staring. It wasn't good manners. I liked good manners. I wished Felix had had them, and Charley's friends, and Conrad Plicker. I never seemed to meet anybody who had good manners.

I went up to my room and began packing. I decided to travel light—just two suitcases, one for my clothes, the other for the money. That money was going to be a pain in the ass, I was sure. I would have been a hell of a lot better off with about ten percent of it. But try parting with a few hundred thousand dollars cash. Just try it. The very thought of it brought apoplexy to my brain, my heart, my kidneys, my bowels, and a tingling to the tips of my fingers.

I left behind most of the nice clothes I'd bought the past few weeks. No way I could carry them. What the hell, wherever I landed all I had to do was walk in somewhere and reoutfit myself. So I just left them hanging in the closet, some of them never having been worn.

I was about to leave when I realized there was still one little question left unanswered: Where was I going? Away from New York. That was all I knew. New York had proven itself definitely unfriendly and was getting less and less subtle about it. Christ, all dressed up, with nearly a half million in my bag, and no place to go.

All right, sweetie, I told myself. What's the thing you can least tolerate? I decided to take that approach, since my pleasures and self-indulgences had brought me nothing but trouble. So what about the opposite? The thing I could least tolerate was being bored. Good, I thought. I was going to be bored—and stay alive.

Chapter Fifteen

I picked Barleyville because it sounded like the place one was most likely to get bored in. Barleyville. Who had ever heard of it? Who would ever go there? Nobody. If I was going to die, let it be in Barleyville, of boredom. A slow death, yes, but who, after all, was in a hurry? Boredom might even prove to be a welcome change, after the years of fun and feathers. Certainly better than a bullet in the back of the head or an automobile in the belly. Good old quiet, peaceful Barleyville. A little main street with trees; Pop's Drug Store, Mom's Restaurant, Buddy's Garage, Sister's Dress Shop, Brother's Hardware. A good town with good people. God bless us one and all.

I was wandering around Penn Station at one in the morning, being ogled by perverts and other demented and drooling citizens of New York. I heard the PA system drone out the roster of stops of the one-twenty now boarding. Some were familiar, like Kingston and Albany, but most sounded like dead ends and Barleyville like the deadest of them all. Ever have a voice call out to you in the middle of the night? Ever have the soft ruffles of the sea wind whisper your name? Well, that's the way Barleyville sounded to me suddenly coming through the loudspeaker in that huge, dreary lobby.

So I headed for that gate, went downstairs to the platform, and boarded the train for Barleyville. There weren't many people in my coach car, just a few sour and sullen-looking guys with loosened tie knots and rolled-up newspapers. I guess people don't like riding trains at that hour; but I can tell you it felt damned good once that train started rolling and I knew I was going to be clear of New York City.

We emerged from the tunnel into the night, the train

moving with quiet, soothing force. The city lights were few and far between at this hour, and my old playground looked more ominous and sinister than ever as it slipped past. Screw you, New York, I thought to myself. You didn't get me. You missed. You tried your damnedest, but you missed. I'd gone right into the wrappers of all your temptations and seductions, swiped my pleasures, and gotten away. Screw you, New York, with all your good times that have to be paid for, sometimes in blood. Here's the little girl that got away. You didn't get me. You lost. My soul belongs to Barleyville.

I got there at three-thirty in the morning. It was damned nice of the train to stop, since I was the only one who got off there. The conductor helped me down the metal steps to the platform.

"Barleyville," he said; I guess he wanted to make sure that I knew where the hell I was getting off.

"Thank you," I said, smiling sweetly, tipping him with a fifty-dollar bill, which he crumpled up in his fist without looking at it, probably figuring it was a buck and who was this hick tipping him for helping her off the train? Boy, was he going to be surprised.

Then the train pulled out and went away. I watched it go off into the night. It raised a long, searching *wooooo-wooooo* into the Hudson River Valley darkness. Christ, there was a sound I'd never heard before. A deprived city girl was I. I'd heard it in the movies, and now here it was in the flesh. To me the sound of somebody gargling phlegm at the next table, the hysterical shrill of fire engines, the thunder of garbage trucks, a fart in a crowded elevator—these had always been the romantic sounds of my life. City sounds. But the *wooooo-wooooo* of that train topped them all. It had character. It had mystery.

The depot was closed. Across the tracks were woods, and they were closed too. I mean there wasn't even a firefly in there. I picked up my two suitcases and walked away from the platform. I crossed a narrow side street and came to Barleyville's main drag. All of those little stores were there, just as I'd suspected, and big old shade trees.

And there was diagonal parking—nothing more small-townish than diagonal parking. When you see diagonal parking you know that everything's all right, that these are good flag-waving, honest, virtuous, apple-pious citizens here. There wasn't a light on anywhere, except for the streetlights and a traffic signal strung up over the middle of the street winking red-orange-green like it was flirting with the night. The main drag was about two blocks long and beyond it I could see houses, modest one-family white clapboards with picket fences around them. Jesus, picket fences! The movies were right—this was what it looked like for real, small-town America.

I sat down on a concrete bench that had wooden slats for seating and backing. Just sat there and waited for something to happen. I got the feeling I might have to sit there for seventy-five years. But that was all right. I'd had enough happen to me lately to hold me for seventy-five years.

But it didn't take seventy-five years. It didn't even take seventy-five minutes. It took about four minutes before I spotted the headlights coming slowly down the curving road beyond the town's business section. I watched the car approach and when it rolled through the red light at the other end of town I knew it had to be police, and I knew they would stop.

It was not a they but a he, and he did stop. The car had County Sheriff lettered on the door. The County Sheriff himself was behind the wheel, wearing a cowboy hat. He parked in front of me, opened the door and got out, leaving his headlights on and his motor running.

"Any problem, ma'am?" he asked. He was standing with one foot up on the curb, giving me one of those studious-curious-dubious looks policemen tend to confront strangers with. They all have it; I guess it's something they learn in cop school: Go stand in front of the mirror for two hours a day, Clancy, until you've got that look down pat; you've not only got to look like a policeman, you've got to *look* like a policeman.

He was a tall, lanky guy, with good biceps in his short-sleeved shirt. He was wearing a holster with a pistol in it and had a badge on his shirt.

"No problem," I said.

That put a furrow in his brow. How could a sexy young thing be sitting out here at three-thirty in the morning and there not be some sort of problem?

"You live around here?" he asked.

"No," I said. "I just got off the train."

"You did?"

"That's right."

"Are you waiting for somebody to pick you up?"

"I don't know anyone around here."

Now he pushed his hat back on his head and grunted. He looked down at the sidewalk while he pondered the situation.

"You just gonna sit here?" he asked.

"No," I said. "Is there a motel nearby?"

"Nearest motel's twenty miles. But there's a rooming house here in town."

"Can we bother them at this hour?"

"Sure," he said. "Mr. Stonehead's used to that."

"Mr. Stonehead?"

That was his name all right, and aptly so. I swear, his head and face looked like they had been carved out of rock. His head was knobby, his face craggy, his eyes pebbly. I got the feeling you could have bounced a hammer off of him and he never would have felt it. He had a little scattering of bristly close-cropped hair that looked like iron filings. He seemed to be around fifty, though it was hard to tell; he could have been a hundred, too.

He came to the door in his bathrobe.

"This is Miss Clem, Hank," the sheriff said.

Hank. Hank Stonehead. Jesus.

"She just got into town and needs a room," the sheriff said.

"Does, eh?" Mr. Stonehead said, looking me over. Those little pebbles lingered on my boobs for a moment.

"Can you fix her up?" the sheriff asked.

"Sure," Mr. Stonehead said.

The sheriff tipped his ten-gallon hat, said good night,

and left me there. I picked up my suitcases and followed Mr. Stonehead inside. He was wearing slippers that made whispery sliding sounds as they went across the carpeting. It was an old house, just outside of town, standing back from the road and hidden by a lot of granddaddy trees. Inside, it was furnished in high-style 1890s, with chandeliers, dull, oversized paintings on the walls, chairs and sofas gluttonous with stuffing, and some potted plants that looked like they had been stolen from the lobby of a hotel on West Forty-seventh Street.

"I'm sorry to bother you at this hour," I said, following my host upstairs, staring at his slippers. They were leather, scrunched down at the back, and his bony white ankles lifted halfway out of them with each step.

"Quite all right," he said without enthusiasm.

The stairway elbowed up from a landing to the second floor. When we got there he opened a wall light, revealing the hallway and four or five closed doors.

"Staying long?" he asked. His voice was kind of distant, indifferent, but I got the feeling he was giving me a lot of thought. He had the oddball habit of closing his eyes when he talked.

"I'm not sure," I said. "It depends."

"On what?" he asked, closing and opening his eyes again. That sort of thing could drive you crackers.

"A lot of things."

He opened a door and showed me into a room, then followed me in and turned on the light. It was a room. Not your flashy modern motel room with wall-to-wall everything, but a reasonably comfortable-seeming arrangement. Big double bed, chairs, chest of drawers, lamps. One wall was bricked up, another had bird lithographs on it. If you were going to die peacefully in your bed, this was the place for it.

I put my bags down on the bed.

"It's six dollars by the day," he said, "or thirty-five by the week. You have the use of the kitchen. The toilet is down the hall." I hadn't heard anybody say toilet in years.

"Why don't we go on a day-by-day basis?" I said. This

would do for a while, until I found out about Barleyville (or until Barleyville found out about me).

"Fine," he said, nodding that rock on his shoulders and closing his eyes while he said it.

"Do you have any other boarders?" I asked.

"They come and go," he said. "Salesmen."

I wondered if there was a Mrs. Stonehead, or any other living thing under this roof. But I figured I'd find out tomorrow, when the sun came up. If I was alone in this place with this creep I didn't want to know about it.

"I'll say good night then, Miss Clem," he said and went out, closing the door after him.

There was no lock on the door, so I pulled a chair over and wedged it in under the doorknob. Then I took off all my clothes, put on a shorty nightgown, and lay down on the bed. The bed felt damp and crinkly. I sure was bedding myself down in strange places this night, starting with good old Felix in Greenwich Village. Boy, that seemed a long time ago.

I couldn't hear a sound. Stonehead had probably crawled back into his crypt. Jeez, what a place. What the hell was I doing there? Staying alive, that's what.

The silence gave me a feeling of aloneness, an in-the-grave sort of aloneness. Not only was the house quiet, but the whole goddamned town. Not a sound. Just a cricket now and then. (Those things *are* crickets, aren't they, with those little *bleep-bleep* sounds?) I lay absolutely still. When it gets that quiet you somehow don't move, as if you don't want to be the one to spoil it. I just lay there, staring at the shadows thrown by the bedside lamp.

What name did I tell the sheriff? Clem. That was it. Fannie Clem. I figured that sounded good for Barleyville. Better not forget it.

I started to cry. Just like that. I'm not an easy sobber, but it came then, in warm little pools in my eyes, then on my eyelids, dripping onto my cheeks. It was the loneliness of it all. I was nobody, and I was nowhere. Nobody in the world gave a damn about me, and there were some who wanted me dead, into the bargain. Christ, every breath I drew was so precious; every minute I stayed alive was like a bonus. People wanted me dead. That was unbelievable; it was unbearable. Me. Of all people. I'd never bothered anybody. All I ever wanted was a good time. How the hell had my life turned into such a monumental fuck-up?

What next? I thought. There I was, in the prime of life, with a suitcase stuffed with money. Lying on a cold old bed in Barelyville, somewhere in the boonies of upstate New York. In a haunted house with Mr. Stonehead. Or was it a house haunted *by* Mr. Stonehead? I was glad the sheriff had brought me there; at least Stonehead wouldn't try to murder me tonight. Christ, Terry, I told myself, cut it out—not *every*body in the world is trying to murder you.

I looked around the room, gazing through tear-dimmed eyes. I sighed. I got under the covers. The sheets felt cold. Goddammit, I thought. Then without even knowing it, I fell asleep.

Chapter Sixteen

Everything looks better by daylight, including Mr. Stonehead's house. It actually looked kind of nice beyond the windows, where the upper boughs of the trees were poised like raised wings.

I got out of bed and put on my robe. I looked in the mirror and took notice of the little dark circles under my eyes. I hadn't been sleeping well lately and it was beginning to show. Christ, I was aging. Christ again, wasn't it bad enough that they were trying to kill me—did they have to age me, too?

Then I pulled the chair away from the door and went down the hall to the "toilet" to clean up. I took a bath in a big old claw-footed tub, letting myself soak in there for nearly an hour. Then I went back to my room, dressed, and went downstairs. There was nobody around. The kitchen looked like it had been scrubbed and polished— there was a gleam to it. The table had a piece of oil cloth on it. Everything was just so, from the glasses lined up on the wooden shelf over the sink to the towels hung in perfect measure on the rack. If this was Stonehead's work then he was a fussy old bastard. I sure as hell wasn't going to make myself anything to eat in this place.

You ever get the feeling, walking into a room, that somebody has just vacated it? That's how I felt as I explored the downstairs of the house, going from the kitchen to the dining room to the living room. Each time I walked into a room I had the feeling he'd just left it.

Finally I looked out the living room window at the back yard and saw him sitting in a chair in the morning sunshine. His back was to me and I had a good long look at that squared-off block that seemed cemented onto his shoulders. It didn't seem human. He was just sitting there, his arms resting on the sides of his aluminum lawn chair.

I decided to walk into town and get some breakfast. It was a nice bright sunny day and the walk felt good. I went about half a mile along a black-topped road, walking under trees most of the time. Now and then a car or a pickup truck passed, fluttering the roadside grass. I suddenly felt good about being there; there was something nice and clean and safe about Barleyville. I felt unthreatened, unafraid.

By the time I reached town I had already decided I'd buy a house here, marry some sterling hunk of local manhood, have children, and grow quietly and boringly old, right here in Barleyville. I didn't miss New York and its brights and glitters at all. To hell with all that phoniness that burns you out before your time. (Of course, I was out of New York so far the grand total of about twelve hours, but I didn't give that little detail too much thought at the moment.)

I picked up a local paper and went into a little restaurant and sat down in the corner at a table with a white cloth on it. It was just after the breakfast hour and a bit before the lunch hour, so the place was virtually empty. There was only me and a couple of waitresses and the cashier. A busboy was setting up the tables for lunch, putting down the place settings and napkins and filling the sugar bowls.

The waitress came over to me. She was a sad-faced, slightly overweight girl of eighteen or nineteen. She walked in kind of a shamble, with an expression on her face that led you to suspect that her every drawn breath was expelled with a little sigh of despair or resignation. She handed me the menu and stood there, little blunt yellow pencil poised to write on a small pad.

"I'd like to study the menu for a moment," I told her. You don't like to have them hovering over you.

"Your earrings are neat," she said.

"What?" I asked, looking up at her. She had a pretty face for all that her cheeks were too round and full and that her blond hair framed her face with idiotic little

138

ringlets; either she had no mirrors in her house or else her hairdresser was a sadist.

"Where'd you buy them, if you don't mind my asking."

"Buy what?" I asked.

"The earrings," she said. "Gee, they're nice."

It so happened they were diamond and had cost me around four or five hundred in a little place in the diamond center, in the West Forties.

"Gee," she said. She was just standing there and staring, her head tilted to one side, her upper lip raised slightly over her front teeth. She looked slightly moronic. I wondered if she might perhaps be having designs upon my ripe and delectable little body—I was kind of leery of undue feminine interest and affection since being jumped on the boat by Helene Corbett. But I immediately felt guilty for thinking it. For God's sake, Terry—your own hangups, your own sordid little mind, dredging up another little cup of cheer from the cesspool of experience.

"You can find them on sale in the diamond center in New York," I said.

"Where?" she asked.

"The diamond center in New York."

"I've never been there."

"You've never been where—the diamond center or New York?"

"Neither," she said.

"Never been in New York?" I asked, unable to hide my amazement.

"Uh-uh."

"You ought to go," I said. "It's the center of the universe."

Listen to me all of a sudden, I thought. Talk about chauvinism. Here I was, spreading the bullshit about a city I couldn't get out of fast enough because it was trying to kill me. But, damnit, it was true: New York *was* the center of it all; it *could* give you an awful lot, if you didn't ask for too much at once. I couldn't believe that this poor kid had never been there. Christ, it was only a few hours away.

"I think it's probably too big for me," she said.

"Nah," I said, sounding very woman-of-the-worldish.

"Well, it's expensive," she said. "People tell me there's no point going to New York unless you can afford it."

"There's probably a lot of truth in that," I said. No question about it. All the same, I got the feeling that people were just trying to scare her away from the city—probably her parents.

"Maybe someday I'll go," she said vaguely. She had a weary voice, like an eighty-year-old. The way she said that made you just know she'd never get to New York, or anywhere else for that matter. Defeat was already there.

"Bring me bacon, scrambled eggs, toast, and coffee," I said.

She wrote it down and shambled away. While I waited for this wild adventurer to return with my breakfast I opened my newspaper. Local news dominated, but on an inside page was an interesting little story out of New York. Two men, it seemed, had been killed when their car broke through an iron guard rail in an all-night garage and plunged to the street below. The story didn't say anything about a strange broad running around without shoes.

Holy Christ, I thought, closing the paper. They'd been killed. Those two bastards had been killed. That made four now—four guys dead trying to kill me. Boy, Charley was probably fit to be tied. If I wasn't so scared of the idea I would have called him, just to see what he had to say. But I couldn't do it. Just the thought of hearing his voice again was enough to make my flesh crawl. Nevertheless, Charley old boy, I thought, even if you do finally get me—which you probably will—you can't say I didn't give you one hell of a run for it. But one thing I made up my mind about—they might get me, but they'd never get that money. If I was going to have any satisfaction out of having my head blown off, that would be it. Spending that goddamned money.

When the waitress returned with my order I said to her, "Quit your job and go to New York."

"I can't," she said.

"Why not?"

"Money."

"I'll give you the money," I said almost nastily. I opened my bag, dug in, and brought out a fistful of bills. Probably around two thousand there, mostly in hundreds. "Take it," I said, thrusting it at her. She was holding my breakfast on a tray.

"I can't," she said.

"Why?" I asked angrily.

"It's a lot of money," she said.

"Of course it is. How else do you think you're going to be able to enjoy New York?"

"But how can I pay it back?"

"Don't worry about it."

"But I don't even know you."

"So what?" I demanded.

Her eyes were fixed upon the money, which I was holding in my tightly clenched fist, the bills sticking out every which way.

"How much is it?" she asked.

"A few thousand."

"Oh, my God," she said, touching her lips with the fingertips of one hand, holding the tray in the other.

"Take it, goddamnit," I said pushing it toward her.

She took a deep breath and then with a gasp said, "I can't."

"Oh, yes you can, and you will," I said. "Put that tray down on the table."

When she did I removed the food and then dumped the money onto the tray.

"Take out two dollars for the breakfast," I said, "and the rest is your tip. Take it and go to New York, for Christ's sake; buy yourself some diamond earrings, have a good time; get yourself a good man, stay there until you've blown all the dough, and then come on back to Barleyville."

She had picked up the tray and was holding it in both hands, her head in a trembling nodding as I spoke, her eyes gazing down at the pile of money.

"Now please leave me alone," I said, picking up my fork and poking at my eggs.

She went away, carrying a trayful of money. A few moments later a rather elegant woman in a gray-checked pants suit appeared at my table. She was around fifty and had apparently made the climb without too much trouble.

"I beg your pardon," she said.

"Why?" I asked.

"Did you just give the waitress all that money?"

I wasn't even looking up; I was staring straight ahead and chewing slowly and with great dignity.

"I did," I said coolly.

"But..."

"I tip for service," I said.

She lingered for several moments. Didn't know what to say. I felt sorry for her. What the hell *could* she say? She *had* to be thinking that I was crackers. Who leaves a two thousand-dollar tip for a two-dollar breakfast?

"Are you aware of how much money you gave the girl?" she asked.

"Quite aware," I said.

She walked away. I was sitting with my back to the action, but I could hear them talking. First in whispers, then growing louder, and then angry and stubborn and getting on toward hysterical.

"Give it back."

"No."

"You can't possibly keep it."

"I can... I can."

"She obviously isn't..."

"She gave it to me!"

"But you can't keep it."

"It's mine... it's mine..."

"It may be stolen."

"I'm keeping it... I'm going to New York."

"Martha... *listen to me!*"

Don't, Martha, I thought. Don't listen. Hang on to it. It's the only chance you'll ever have.

When I got up to leave they became quiet. There were three of them standing at the cash register—Martha, the newly endowed waitress, the fancy woman, and another woman, who looked at me with wide-eyed horror as I passed.

142

Outside, I started to laugh. Christ, money could be fun, if you didn't take it too seriously. Then I realized I had done a foolish thing: if I wanted to live in this town quietly and inconspicuously, handing out two thousand-dollar tips to waitresses wasn't the way to go about it. Good old Terry, as sober and responsible as ever.

I walked around town for a while, going in and out of stores, smiling at everybody. I felt relaxed, unafraid, and it was a damned nice feeling, for a change. This was Small Townsville, USA, all right. It had all the right little stores, trees on the main street, a movie that didn't open until seven o'clock at night, a little green park right in the middle of town.

People seemed friendly, polite, and content to mind their own business. There wasn't even dog shit on the sidewalks. I don't know what the dogs did with it, but they didn't leave it underfoot. Not like in New York, where some mornings you can almost ski to the subway. Quiet, sweet-smelling Barleyville. I loved it. The place I'd been looking for since ... since ... well, since yesterday.

Chapter Seventeen

When I got back to the rooming house there was a guy sitting on the porch. He looked pretty comfortable there, slouched in a rocker, feet up on the railing. I figured he was a boarder.

He was staring at me as I came up the steps, which didn't surprise me, since I was wearing a snug blouse and a short skirt that revealed a lot of shapely panty-hosed thigh as I came up the steps. I stared right back at him. That was the way to do it: if they had it, staring would bring it out; it lets the guy know he's been noticed. I didn't mind noticing him. He was kind of cute, about twenty-five, with yellow farmboy hair which grew down to the collar of his plaid farmboy shirt, the sleeves of which he had rolled back to show his good strong arms. He was wearing khakis and loafers, and I noticed he had no socks on.

I stopped at the head of the steps and he smiled, a big, roguish smile, like he'd just watched his pig eat my pig.

"Good afternoon, Miss Clem," he said.

Jeez, the name threw me for a second. I'd forgotten it. Fannie Clem. That's who I was.

"I'm Ben Josephson," he said.

"Are you living here?" I asked.

"No," he said, "but I'm considering moving in right now."

"Want me to help you pack?" I asked. Might as well give this hick a little shocker right off the bat, I thought.

He laughed, a little uneasily, staring at me as if trying to size me up.

"Where you from?" he asked.

"Why?" I asked, feeling a bit defensive; after all, I

couldn't forget there were still people looking to do a number on me.

"It's a legitimate question," he said.

"I guess it is."

"Don't tell me if you don't want to."

"Well, thank you," I said.

"But at the same time, don't blame me for being curious."

"So far I'm not blaming you for anything," I said.

"Thank heavens," he said. "I wouldn't want to start our friendship with recriminations."

I sat down on the top step now, resting my back against the post at the head of the stairs, trying for as much dignity as my short skirt would allow.

"I work for the *Patriot*," he said.

"Who's the patriot?" I asked. I honestly thought he was referring to a person.

"That's our newspaper. Barleyville *Patriot*."

"You're a newspaperman?"

He nodded. "Don't I look like one?"

"No, as a matter of fact," I said. "You look like a guy who's out of work."

He threw back his head and laughed. "That's just my casual nature," he said. "Right now I'm working very hard, believe me."

"What are you doing here?" I asked.

"I wanted to ask you a few questions."

Christ, I thought. Small towns. He'd probably already heard that I'd given that waitress the two grand and now here he was wanting to know why and what. Charley had never liked newspapermen and for a long time that was my attitude too. Charley's attitudes had been my attitudes.

"Like what?" I asked.

"Well, I heard that a beautiful young woman had turned up in town at three-thirty in the morning with no place to go. In Barleyville that's big news."

So that's why he was there. If he thought that was news, wait till he heard what the new girl in town had done at the restaurant.

"Do you investigate every new person who comes to town?" I asked.

"Only the lookers," he said.

Boy, this is just what I needed. A story about me and my money in a yokel newspaper.

"Listen," I said, "I'm not looking to be a celebrity. I just want to be left alone."

"That's the last thing in the world you should tell a newspaperman."

"Well, if you want to be my friend, then you ought to pay attention."

"I sure want to be your friend, Miss Clem."

I was glad he said the name again; I kept forgetting it. Fannie Clem. Christ, did I look like a Fannie Clem?

When I went upstairs he followed me, chattering away about nothing. Stonehead wasn't around—for which Ben Josephson seemed grateful—and we went up to my room. The next thing I knew we were wrestling around on the bed, kind of playful. I must be an engraved invitation to men; he just went at it, kissing me, holding me firmly, and then all of a sudden he was groping under my little skirt. I resisted just enough to maintain my self-respect.

"Listen," I said, "I'm a virgin."

"I don't believe it," he said. He has his hand cupped under my crotch, where I was getting hot and moist through my little silk panties. "I feel too much experience down there."

"Aren't you afraid of insulting me?" I asked.

He answered that with a soul kiss. There was nothing polished about this guy, but he was strong and self-assured. I got the impression he'd gained his experience in the back seats of parked cars in lovers' lanes. I kept him from rolling down my panties for almost ten minutes while he grunted and gasped. Finally he said, with some consternation in his voice, "Look, I'm going to come in ten seconds ... give me a break."

I couldn't fight that. It was a brand-new approach, for me. So I threw my arms aside and lay back. He drew my legs together, put one hand behind my knees, and lifted me up while he pulled down my panties. He was in a

God-awful hurry; he didn't even take off his pants, just yanked down his zipper and that thing came shooting out like a jack-in-a-box, quivering and yearning to drive itself home. I'd never been screwed by a guy who was wearing his pants. But in a minute I saw why he hadn't taken them off—he didn't have time. I swear it wasn't more than a half dozen strokes before he brought himself off. The guy went wild, like he was being hit with electric shocks.

When it was over he lay on top of me gasping, trying to calm himself.

"That was some rabbit act," I said.

"I'm sorry," he said ruefully.

"When was the last time—when you were fifteen?"

"No," he said. "That's not it. It's you. I've never seen anyone like you." He sounded sincere, he said it very simply, and I had to believe him, considering the dispatch with which he'd blasted off.

He got up and undressed. It was the first time I'd ever had anyone undress after screwing. Then he finished undressing me. He started kissing my breasts, then slid down and licked my belly. I thought he might go all the way—I hadn't had a tongue down there since good old Helene Corbett, who had been everything I could have desired except the right sex. But he didn't, though the thought of it had started me squirming.

Then he took my hand and placed it under his balls while he kneeled over me. I caressed and tickled with the pads of my fingers and in about thirty seconds he was ready again. He pushed in gently and slowly. This time it was lovely, for both of us. It was as if the first time he had simply been checking to see if his gun could fire. He was a nice, smooth, considerate lay. Made me just sink into myself and forget everything. A hell of a trick, all things considered.

"This was her room," he was saying later. We were still lying in bed. The blinds were closed. It was about seven o'clock now and the room was in twilight. Stonehead was in the house—we'd heard him come in—but now the place was quiet. Ben had begun talking about some girl he'd known who had lived there two years before. I wasn't paying that much attention; it wasn't the sort of topic you much care about when you're lying naked together in bed. Her name was Gretchen.

"She came down from Utica for a job here," Ben was saying. "Nice kid. About nineteen. Pretty. Different sort from you."

I heard that all right. "What's that supposed to mean?"

"Shy. Not worldly. You're worldly."

"You mean I fuck."

"That's not what I mean. She wasn't sophisticated. Had a very strict upbringing. Wouldn't even let me come upstairs to her room."

"Boy, she didn't know what she was missing," I said. I liked the feel of this guy's arms around me. "Or did she?"

"It was a platonic relationship," he said. "It probably would have grown into something more, but then she disappeared."

"What do you mean, disappeared?" I asked.

"Just what it says: here one day, gone the next."

"Well, where?"

"Nobody knows. She never went back home—her family never heard from her. As far as I know, nobody ever heard from her."

"Doing her thing, I suppose," I said dreamily. She had probably gotten tired of him not screwing her. But I really didn't care. I was palming his pecker, trying to bring it to life again. He brushed my hand away. "You're not very tactful, Ben-boy," I said. "After what we've been doing all afternoon, you start talking about another broad."

"This was her room," he said.

"So she packed up and walked out on you. That's a hell of a broad to be mooning over."

He was quiet for a few minutes, then in an odd little voice said, "She never packed up."

"What do you mean?"

"Everything was still here, all her belongings. Everything."

"How do you explain that?"

"How do you explain it?" he asked right back.

148

I could give him a theory. Hell, I'd done the same thing, more or less, when I checked out of the hotel in New York. They're probably still wondering about Miss—Christ, I couldn't even remember the name I'd given them—who'd checked out and left most of her belongings behind.

"Women do peculiar things sometimes," I said.

"True; but not this one. She wasn't the type."

"How long did you know her?"

"A few months."

"Were you in love with her?" Big important question.

He shrugged. "I don't know. But I liked her a lot; she was a very fine person."

"Nobody saw her leave?"

"Uh-uh."

"Was she in any trouble?"

"No. She minded her business. I was one of her few friends in town. She didn't socialize much."

"So what happened? What did you do about it?"

"I ran a few stories in the paper, and that got people curious. Stonehead got mad as hell about it, because the police came around to question him, and then to search the place."

"Don't tell me they thought he done her in?" I asked.

"Nobody knew what to think. I organized the Scout troop to search the woods, then got the state police to drag the lake."

"Come on," I said. "You thought she was murdered?"

"It was a possibility. People don't just disappear."

"Sure they do," I said, thinking of sweet little Terry, who was trying to accomplish just that.

"Not without good reason they don't," he said.

"Maybe she had a good reason."

"Maybe," he said, without conviction.

I began to get a queasy feeling. I was in her room, her bed. The room started to feel awfully sinister.

"What about Stonehead?" I asked. "You think he had something to do with it?"

"She said he'd made a pass at her once. I told her to get

out of here, and I think she was considering it. Then she disappeared."

"Was she afraid of him?"

"I don't think so. But she didn't like him."

"Then what the hell am I doing here?" I asked aloud, though the question was more for myself.

"I don't know. What *are* you doing here?"

I knew he meant Barleyville, not the house.

"It's a long story, Ben."

"You in trouble?"

"The crime syndicate is trying to kill me."

"No, seriously," he said. "Are you in trouble?"

See? Tell the truth and nobody believes you. What would he have said if I told him there was about $475,000 in that suitcase over there?

"I'm trying to live on my own for a while," I said.

"You married?"

"No. You?"

"Hell of a question, under the circumstances. But I'm not."

"Good," I said snuggling against him. His armpit had a good, strong man-smell.

"You going to stay in Barleyville?"

"Maybe. If nobody bothers me."

"Nobody's going to bother you here," he said.

"Don't be so sure. I had breakfast this morning and left the waitress a two thousand-dollar tip so she could go to New York."

He laughed. Boy, you just couldn't tell the truth anymore.

"I don't want that in the paper though," I said.

"Don't worry," he said.

Christ, how was I going to explain that? Of all the dumb things I'd done in my life, that took the cake. That took the whole bakery.

"Listen," he said, "I'd rather you didn't stay on in this house."

"Why?"

"Stonehead. He's a weird son of a bitch. I don't like him. I think he's a bit touched."

"Who else lives here?"

"Nobody. He's always been a loner. He lived here with a sister, a maiden sister, until she died. Now he's here by himself, except for a few salesmen who stay now and then for a night. But I don't like the idea of you being here alone with him."

"You think he's dangerous?"

"My father knew him as a kid. He said Stonehead was always strange, that once he was accused of molesting a little girl when he was a young man. I think he's sexually warped. Having you in the house could send him around the bend."

"You think that's what happened to the other girl? That he made a move, she resisted, he got angry and done her in?"

"I don't like to say."

"But you think it."

"I don't know what to think," he said. He was pretty tense now. "I just don't know why a girl would walk out in the middle of winter and leave all her belongings behind and never been seen again."

"What was Stonehead's explanation?" I asked.

"He had none. Shrugs, don't know's, blank looks. Nobody could pin a thing on him. The guy's whole life has been a secret."

"I didn't know you had these weirdies in small towns."

"Are you kidding?" he grunted. "The woodwork's full of them."

"I came here for peace and quiet."

"Oh, you'll find that here, in great abundance. I think that's what drives them off the deep end. Proportionately, you'll find more nuts here than you will in the big city."

"That's hard to believe," I said.

"It's true."

"So why do you stay here?"

"Born here," he said with a little sigh that was half regret, half satisfaction.

"You can leave."

"I've only given you the negative side," he said. "It also has its attractive side. I like fishing and hunting, the outdoors. Things like that. I don't think I could ever live in a city. And I like being a small-town reporter. Just not very ambitious, I guess."

"Stay that way," I said.

"I think that's why I was drawn to Gretchen. We both liked the peace and quiet here. We could walk in the woods or take a canoe out on the lake and not say a word to each other for hours. If you can communicate affection and regard through silence, you've really got something going for you. You're close to the real thing."

"She sounds like a nice person," I said. I don't know if she did or not, but I felt I ought to say it.

"She sure was," he said with quiet emphasis. "I guess she was an introvert. But that was all right. I'm something of that myself, believe it or not."

"How can you be an introvert and a pushy reporter at the same time?"

"Dual personality," he said with a laugh. "Anyway, I'm not really a pushy reporter—there's nothing around here to be pushy about. Nothing ever happens. I cover weddings, funerals, picnics, christenings, high school athletic events. Nothing ever happens here."

"But a girl disappeared."

"That's right."

"She could have gone out and got zonked by some pervert in the woods," I said.

"It was the middle of winter, sweetheart," he said. "Nobody was walking in the woods, not Gretchen and not the perverts. Do you know what winters are like here? It's like living in the bowels of an iceberg."

"So what did she do with herself? Didn't she have any friends besides you?"

"No, just some casual acquaintances. I guess I was her only real friend."

"Then you must have been the chief suspect," I said, which was a lovely remark to make to a naked man who had his fingers two inches from my throat.

"Thanks a lot," he said. "But for your information, I was off on a three-day fishing weekend in the Adirondacks with friends when she disappeared."

"Where was Stonehead?"

"He was here. His story was he didn't know anything. She came home from work Friday night and nobody ever saw her again."

"But what the hell did she do with herself?"

"Nothing much. On winter nights, when we weren't together, she used to sit up here and . . ."

He stopped talking. He looked around and then I swear a shock of tension or awareness or something went through him and he sat bolt upright, so fast he knocked me aside.

"Good Christ!" he whispered.

"What's the matter?" I asked, whispering too. Why is it when one person whispers the other one does too?

He didn't say anything except that he would be right back. He threw his clothes on in a hurry and went flying out of there like his ass was on fire.

Chapter Eighteen

I didn't know what it was all about. I got up and put my clothes on, opened my money bag to make sure it was still all there—it was—and then closed it again. Christ, Terry, I thought, is this the peace and quiet you were after?—going to bed with a guy in the bed of his girl friend who had disappeared and maybe been murdered in the very bed? Oh, shit, I thought.

I don't know why I remembered it, but all of a sudden my mind went back to one day in high school. The school had declared a program of Flower Help. We spent the spring and summer growing flowers in the school garden, and then we were going to pick them and sell them and give the money to the Heart Fund. I was in charge of the petunias. I had my goddamned petunias all picked and boxed and everything, but instead of going out with the other kids to sell them, I went into the boys' room with one of the school jocks and started fooling around. I'd never been in a boys' bathroom before and it was all very daring and exciting and erotic (I had a lot of class in those days). Then he wanted a hand job. I didn't give him one, but he came anyway, while he was feeling me up. He had my dress up over my head and his hands halfway up my ass when a teacher walked in.

We were hauled down to the principal's office, naturally. Everybody always has to make a big thing out of everything. The principal was a woman—a Miss, no less, a Miss Delilah Feeney, who was about fifty-five years old, and you just *knew* nobody had ever put their hands up *her* ass, or even on her shoulder, for that matter. She gave me a lecture about my behavior, telling me the school was not a place of moral freedom, that I was not at liberty to indulge my "prurient instincts within these walls." She said one other thing I always remembered: "You should have sold petunias."

I don't know why I thought of that now, but there it was again, coming back at me: Why the goddamned hell didn't I sell my petunias?

When he came back Ben was carrying a toolbox, muttering something about always having one in the trunk of his car. He put it down on the bed, where our warm behinds had been just a few minutes before.

"Excuse me, Ben," I said. He was so involved in what he was doing—rummaging through the toolbox—that he didn't hear me. "Excuse me, Ben," I said, louder.

He looked around, an expression of wild excitement in his face. He was holding a hammer in one hand and a sharp-edged steel chisel in the other. I was wondering whether he might have cracked up all of a sudden. I wouldn't have been surprised; my track record for picking winners wasn't so hot.

"What?" he asked.

"Humor me," I said. "Tell me what's going on."

He looked at the door; it was shut. But it had been a nervous glance. When he spoke it was in a whisper.

"I'm so stupid sometimes it's almost charming," he said. "It just sank into me what Gretchen said. One of the reasons she liked living in this place was because of the fireplace; she said she could spend hours sitting here on a winter's night, just staring into the fire."

"So what?" I asked.

He gave me a sly smile.

"Do you see a fireplace in here?" he asked.

I didn't. "Maybe she sat in another room," I said.

"She said *her* room."

"But . . ."

"Look at that."

He was pointing at the wall, where it was bricked up.

"That's where it was," he said.

"Okay," I said. "So what?"

"I'm going to find out for sure," he said. That was why he had those tools in his hands.

"You're going to knock those bricks out?" I asked.

155

"Damn right."

"Just to prove that there used to be a fireplace there?"

I still didn't get it, still didn't lock into his thinking. He went over to the bricked-up wall and began examining it, running his fingers across the bricks as though looking for a weak spot. I was going to ask what was so important about proving there had been a fireplace there, when all of a sudden it struck me: he wasn't just looking for a fireplace—he was looking for that girl's body.

He set the chisel's cutting edge against the wall and began tapping on it with the hammer.

"Hey, for Christ's sake," I whispered. "He's in the house—he'll hear you."

"The hell with him," he said.

I went over to the door and wedged the chair under the knob. It wasn't going to take long for Stonehead to get up there. Then I sat down in a chair where I could see the door and watch Ben at the same time. He was crouched at the wall, tapping away slowly and steadily, sending a little stream of brick dust to the floor.

"It's coming," he said.

"What about Stonehead?" I asked.

"The hell with him."

"It's *his* house."

But he wasn't paying much attention to me; in fact, he wasn't paying *any* attention to me. I just sat there and listened to that steady *tap-tap-tap* of the hammer upon the chisel, wondering how long it was going to take for the message to reach whatever dark corner Stonehead sat in. I wished there was some noise in this place to give Ben a little cover, but there wasn't a sound.

"He did a lousy job on this," Ben said. "Must've been in a big hurry. The son of a bitch," he muttered. He obviously was convinced that he was going to find what he expected to.

A body stuffed in there? If there was I didn't want to see it. Boy, I thought, I sure as hell wasn't sleeping another night in here, no matter which way it came up.

He kept tapping away until he had knocked out a brick. Another soon followed. I was getting more and more uneasy, as much as from the idea of a body lying behind that wall as from the thought of Stonehead coming in.

"It's hollow back there all right," Ben said. "Why should he have put up a wall here? I'll tell you why. The son of a bitch. Goddamnit, I wish I had a sledgehammer."

Then I heard footsteps on the stairs.

"Ben," I whispered, "he's coming!"

"Good," he said not missing a beat on that wall. "Just the man I want to see."

"You crazy bastard; suppose he's got a gun?"

"Lock the door."

"I already have."

There was a knock on the door.

"Miss Clem?"

I thought Ben would stop then, to try and fake Stonehead away. But he didn't. He was absolutely obsessed; he kept tap-tap-tapping away at that wall like a guy sending a last shot of Morse code to the outside world while the Russians are breaking down the door.

"Miss Clem, what is going on in there?" Stonehead sounded anxious, and I was willing to bet that this time he was keeping his eyes open while he talked.

Hell, I figured, if Ben didn't care, I surely didn't. Why add a lie to my already overlong catalogue of sins?

"Mr. Josephson is knocking down your brick wall," I said.

When I said that, Ben wheeled around in his crouch and looked at me like I'd gone positively zocko.

"That's gonna hit the fan at ninety miles an hour, you crazy bastard," he said.

Stonehead didn't say anything, just stood outside the door.

Ben started tapping again and broke off two more bricks; they seemed to be coming easily now. Stonehead struck the door a couple of pretty heavy blows, then tried the knob.

"Open this door," he said. There was a calm in his voice that was scary.

Ben took a pencil flashlight out of his toolbox and flashed it through the opening he'd made, craning his neck as he moved the light around behind the wall. When he turned around I could see it in his face—he looked like he was going to vomit. Unable to say anything, he stared at me with a most piteous expression. Then the noise at the door seemed to command his attention for the first time and he glared over in that direction. I didn't budge, sitting there like my ass was frozen to the chair. Then, with a gesture of violent anger he threw down the tools and went striding across the room toward the door with a lunatic look in his face.

And then they killed each other, Sheriff. I could hear myself telling it now.

You saw it happen?

With my own little baby blues.

What were you doing there?

I'd come there for peace and quiet.

Why did they kill each other?

Because there was a body behind the wall.

A body, miss?

A body, you bet. A body.

And what were you doing while they were killing each other, miss?

Wishing I'd sold petunias.

Ben kicked the chair from the door and yanked it open. I expected to see Stonehead standing there with a shotgun. But he didn't have a shotgun. He didn't have anything in his hands except two fists. If Ben's face was wild, Stonehead's was wilder. Ben reached out, grabbed him by the shirtfront, pulled him into the room, spun him around, and threw him onto the bed.

"You degenerate son-of-a-bitching bastard!" Ben yelled.

Stonehead was snarling; I swear, steam was coming out of his ears and nose. He tried to get up but Ben pushed him down again.

"You've desecrated my house," Stonehead whispered.

"I . . . I . . ." Ben spluttered. He couldn't talk, he was so furious, but finally got out: "*I* desecrated it?"

Stonehead threw a hysterical glance at the brick wall and its telltale little opening, then looked back to Ben.

"You should leave the dead in peace," he said.

"You should leave the living in peace!" Ben yelled. He looked as if in another minute he was going to go clear out of his head.

That's when the second commotion started, from downstairs. All of a sudden a woman's voice was yelling for Mr. Stonehead, full of fury and demand—a marching chorus of righteousness.

"Mr. Stonehead!" she yelped. "*Mist*er Stonehead!"

That brought the matter to a halt, temporarily, and I yelled out, "Up here!" Shit, if there was going to be a murder here—*another* murder, I should say—I didn't want to be the only witness.

A moment later a fat woman burst into the doorway, her round melon of a face bright red, her chins bobbing. She was wearing a lumber jacket and blue jeans that contained a can that looked like the back of a Madison Avenue bus. She strode into the room like a field marshal and I stopped wondering who she was and what it was all about when I saw who was cowering timidly behind her. Oh, God, I moaned just loud enough for myself to hear. It was my little waitress, the one I'd given the unholy tip to. She had a little ball of handkerchief in her fist. When she saw me she gave me a shy smile. Her eyes were red.

"Mr. Stonehead," the woman said, after scowling at me. "Who is this woman?"

"What?" Stonehead asked. The guy looked almost human in his puzzled curiosity.

"I demand to know who this woman is and what she's after."

Poor Ben. He was the one to feel sorry for. Here he'd finally solved the mystery, was about to have the joy of pulverizing the culprit, and now *this* had to happen.

"Please, Mrs. Sylvester . . ." he said.

But Mrs. Sylvester was having none of him.

"Mind your business, Mr. Josephson," she boomed out in a voice thick with menace. Mind your business or else I'll put one right on your chops—that was her message.

"*This* woman," she said to Stonehead, jerking her thumb at me, "is some sort of blackguard or spy or pervert or something."

The waitress was still smiling at me with shy love and admiration. *She* knew I was okay.

"What are you talking about?" Ben asked.

Mrs. Sylvester looked at him like he smelled like a skunk. Stonehead tried to get up but Ben shoved him back down. This made an impression on Mrs. Sylvester.

"This woman, Mr. Josephson," the lady said to Ben (getting, I guess, the message that Ben was in charge here, not Stonehead, and so giving the explanation to him), "came out of the blue this morning and gave my Martha two thousand dollars, for no good reason. I want to know what's behind it."

Now Ben looked at me, no doubt remembering what I'd said earlier about that. The poor guy didn't know what to make of it. He'd laughed when I had told him; he wasn't laughing now.

"I want to know what she wants from my daughter," Mrs. Sylvester said.

"I don't want anything from your daughter," I said.

"Is it your habit to go around tipping waitresses thousands of dollars?" the fat lady demanded.

"I think you ought to know, Mrs. Sylvester," I said, "that there's a dead body behind that wall."

"There's going to be another one there soon if I don't get an answer," she said. "What's your game, sister? Who are you?"

"Fannie," Ben said. "What's this all about?"

"The girl wanted to go to New York," I said. That was the truth, but truth didn't seem to be going very far at the moment: Mrs. Sylvester, for instance, hadn't even *looked* at the brick wall when I told her there was a body behind it.

"I'm calling the police," she said.

That rang a bell with Stonehead, I guess—that sound of "police"—because all of a sudden he was up and running. Ben whirled and grabbed him and they went wrestling together, like two drunks trying to waltz. They swung around and smacked flush into Mrs. Sylvester, knocked her on her considerable ass, and then fell on top of her,

160

while Martha-the-waitress-who-wanted-to-go-to-New York started to scream.

Terry, I said to myself, *now!* I jumped up, grabbed the money suitcase, and bolted out of there, leaving all the yelling and thumping behind. I ran down the stairs and dashed outside, with one sight indelibly fixed in my mind: the sight of Mrs. Sylvester's white drawers showing through the splitting seams of her jeans as she took her flop on the floor.

I ran to Ben's car, saw he had left the keys in the ignition—these wonderful trusting crime-free small-towners, bless 'em—and got in and started her up. I made a U turn and headed away from there. I kept going until I hit a crossroad and stayed on that until I saw signs for a highway. I followed them, got onto the highway, and drove for about a hundred miles (staying under the speed limit; I'd had enough for one night) until I was exhausted. I pulled into the next motel I saw and checked in.

I bolted my door behind me and dropped onto the bed as if I didn't have a bone in my body. *Jeezuss,* I thought: a crazy landlord, a body behind the wall, a crazy woman. All I'd wanted was some peace and quiet. The fat son of a bitch, I thought, tenderly, about Mrs. Sylvester. With all the yipping about the money, I still didn't hear her offering to hand it back. Hypocritical old bitch. So I'd ended up giving *her* the two grand. Sorry, Charley.

I opened up the money bag, looked at it, and just shook my head. And, Christ, I was going to have to buy clothes again. This running away on the fly all the time was getting inconvenient.

I fell asleep without getting undressed. I didn't want to take those clothes off; hell, they were all I had.

The next morning I called a taxi and arranged to be driven to the Albany airport. The dispatcher said it would be expensive. "Don't bore me with that, please," I said airily. Then I put in a call to Ben at the Barleyville *Patriot.*

"So you got your man," I said to him when he came to the phone.

"Where the hell are you?" he demanded. "Where's my car?"

"Wait a minute," I said. "First tell me what happened. I left at a crucial moment."

He sighed. "Stonehead's in the lock-up."

"Was she really behind that wall?"

"Yes," he said soberly.

"Did you have much trouble after I left?"

"Well, sort of. I've got a broken hand."

"You mean he almost got away?"

"He was doing his damnedest. But then Mrs. Sylvester kicked him in the balls."

"She did?" I smiled. Good old Mrs. Sylvester.

"Now listen," he said, but I cut him off.

"I can't give you any answers," I said. "I'm sorry, Ben, but I can't."

"I clear up one mystery and now you're going to start another?"

"I can't help it."

"You're in trouble, aren't you?"

"Yep."

"Can't I help?"

"Nope."

"Will you be all right?" he asked.

"Sure," I said.

"What's your real name?"

"I don't know anymore." I felt tears start to my eyes. This was a real nice guy. And I was going to have to forsake him.

"Fannie Clem," he said. "You'll always be Fannie Clem to me."

"A hell of a name, isn't it?"

"Will you come back one day?" he asked.

"No."

"Will you let me know from time to time that you're all right?"

"No," I said, shaking my head. The tears were really rolling now.

"Okay," he said. "I understand. But if ever..."

"If ever, yes."

162

"I'll hang on to that then," he said.

When I saw the cab pull up outside I told him where he could find his car, then apologized for having taken it.

"I'll tell them you'll be picking it up," I said.

"I won't ask any questions when I get there," he said.

"Bless you," I said and hung up.

Then I went out and got into the cab and headed for the airport. Where to now? I asked myself.

Chapter Nineteen

I'll tell you where to, and I'll tell you why, too. I had tried the small town, right? All right, I was there for only a day, but wasn't that enough? Jesus, in one day I had Mr. Stonehead, a walled-up pile of bones for a roommate, and then Mrs. Sylvester. That was just *one day's* entertainment. Should I have stayed another day? What about a week? A month? Can you possibly imagine what could have happened in a month? At least in big bad bloody sinful New York I'd had two unbothered weeks before those creepies had spotted me in the Village.

I don't have anything against small towns; in fact, Barleyville was as pretty a place as you could ask. But let's be realistic: a small town is no place for a softly curved young thing with a healthy libido and hundreds of thousands of dollars in a suitcase. Add to that a want of good sense and discretion, and you have somebody who will stand out in a small town like a flagpole in a canoe. I couldn't help it. I wasn't built for small-town virtues, I was built for big-city pleasures and vices. Either you have that kind of pilot light or you don't. I did and there was no sense fighting it.

I have parents and cousins and aunts and uncles who have spent their lives floating like lily pads on stagnant waters. Nothing has ever happened to them or because of them. Statues have had more adventurous lives. Me, I'm just the opposite. I can't walk out the front door without something happening. And this is minding my own business. People have never learned to keep away from me. Poor Ben Josephson; I did him the biggest favor possible in running away. Look what happened to him in just one day. Okay, it worked out all right, but, hell, Stonehead could just as easily have come in there with a shotgun and killed him.

I remembered Cliffie Schickleman. He had a crush on me in high school and I went out with him because he wasn't a bad guy. Shy and nervous; never touched me. Once in the movies I took his hand and placed it on the inside of my thigh. He was so startled and got so wrought up that he vomited. Splattered all over a blond pony tail in the row in front of us. Some tribute to my charms, eh?

Then one of the jocks—the guy who had lifted up my dress in the boys' room when I should have been selling my petunias—warned Cliffie to keep away. I was staked-out territory, it seemed. That ticked me off and *I* started calling Cliffie for dates. Finally the jock got sore. One night him and some of his ape friends grabbed Cliffie and brought him up to the building where I lived. They dragged him to our apartment door, pulled down his pants and underwear, bent him over, tied his wrists to his ankles, stuck a dandelion in his ass, rang the bell, and went away.

Boy, I'll never forget that. I was sitting in the living room watching television with the whole family. My father got up to answer the door. He came back a minute later, a baffled look on his face.

"Who was it?" my mother asked.

"There's a boy standing out there with a flower in his behind," he said.

"Louis," my mother said angrily. Shocking. My sisters started to laugh. I half believed him; my father never was one for joking.

"Look for yourself," my father said.

My mother screwed up the corner of one eye and stared menacingly at him. You didn't fool with my mother. She got up, went to the door, opened it, gasped, and slammed it shut. The next thing we heard was her dialing the police.

"Police?" she said. "There is a person standing in my hallway with a flower in his behind." And then: "I *assure* you I am serious."

That convinced the rest of us and we all made a beeline for the door, but my father got there first and wouldn't let us open it. Then a neighbor came along, deflowered Cliffie so to speak, untied him, and that was that. When the police came my mother indignantly denied having made the call. Nobody was going to sucker her into making a sap of herself, she told us.

Cliffie never spoke to me again.

Anyway, that's one of the things that happened.

So I went to Las Vegas. That's right. The heart of Charleyland. Foolhardy? Stupid? Crazy? Maybe. But maybe that would be the last place they'd think of looking for me. But I had to go *somewhere*, didn't I? I couldn't ride in a taxi cab for the rest of my life, even though I could afford it. If they were going to get me at least let me enjoy myself before it happened. What point was there in vegetating in some hick town and rotting with boredom and then maybe getting shot in the head anyway? I had all that money and I was damned if I wasn't going to have my jollies before they got me.

If it's an unreal life you're leading then it's to an unreal place that you ought to go. And nothing is less real than Vegas. I'd been there with Charley a few times and found it absolutely unbelievable. Twenty-four hours, around the clock, always going, like it's afraid to stop even for a minute, as though it would all come crashing down if it did.

I actually felt a little surge of defiant pride as I deplaned and walked through the dry, simmering sunshine to the terminal, because I had stopped running away. Christ, you can't be very proud of yourself if you're running and hiding all the time. This whole crazy maneuver made me feel strangely exhilarated, although I can't say I would have been happy to see a couple of Charley's goons hanging around someplace.

I took a cab to one of the town's better hotels and booked myself into a fifty-dollar-a-day room, paying ten days in advance with hard cash (that was thinking positively, Terry, old girl, I told myself: ten days). I used the name Audrey DeLand, which I thought was pretty nice. I'd made it up on the plane while listening to a German journalist babbling away about his impressions of America. He wasn't a bad-looking guy but his accent turned me off, especially when he kept pronouncing the "b" in plumber while telling me some endless story about a john that wouldn't stop flushing. I told him my name was Hildegarde Heinkel, just to make him feel at home, while deciding to become Audrey DeLand.

The first thing I did after checking into the hotel was go out and buy myself another wardrobe. I went for a lot of splashy colorful stuff, plus a couple of evening gowns, spending around two grand. Then I went and had my hair touched up, tipping a French fag a hundred bucks for the job, for which he almost collapsed in tears.

I spent the first night in my room, ordering room service, and then watching TV, and then counting my money. I had around $460,000 left. Spending like a lunatic, I'd still barely scratched the surface of that bankroll.

The hotel had a brochure in the room listing what was going on around town, who was where and that sort of thing. A lot of big names were performing but I didn't want to take too many crazy chances, so I didn't make any reservations. But I did notice the name of a small-time singer I'd met a few times when I was with Charley—Johnny Blake. We'd seen him here in Vegas once and another time in Miami. Charley seemed to know him fairly well and hinted once that he'd had a hand in getting the guy some gigs here and there. Johnny was always very respectful around Charley, though I couldn't help getting the impression that he resented having to be. There was something gentle and sensitive about him that I liked.

Johnny was working a small room in a good hotel, along with a comic I'd never heard of. Johnny was never going to be big-time, which somehow seemed to suit him—he didn't have that on-the-make obnoxious ambitious drive that a lot of performers did; he never showed you a thousand teeth when he smiled. He seemed content to sing his quiet ballads and then fade away at the end of a show. I decided I'd go hear him the next night.

I walked around town the next day and whenever I passed a mirror had a look. I swear my mother wouldn't have recognized me, with my phony blond hair in an upsweep and my Foster Grants hiding half my face. I felt good; these were my surroundings, this was where I belonged. I had the crazy notion that nobody could hurt me here. From here I'd go to L.A. for a while, then maybe to Honolulu; and when the season started go on to Miami and Nassau. Atta girl, Terry, just keep up that positive thinking.

That night I dolled up and went to hear Johnny sing. He was working a small, dark, smoky room. They gave me a table near the small stage and I had dinner while the comic machine-gunned thirty minutes of one-liners, some of which were funny. Then Johnny came on, working under a spot, as usual accompanied by a slow, tinkly piano, to sing his heartbreak ballads.

He was a tall, thin kid—I always thought of him as a kid even though he was about thirty; he just had that way about him. He worked in a white silk shirt open at the throat and tight black pants—that was his costume. He had a long, sad face and big round eyes that seemed filled with suffering and which went just great with his throaty-voiced ballads, which he sang from a wooden bar stool. Audiences liked him; you never heard a sound in the room when he sang. Charley always took my hand and squeezed it when Johnny sang. Maybe that's why I was there, hungering for a little of the old familiar; not sentimental about Charley, certainly, but just to renew some tie, no matter how slender, to the old life.

I never thought Johnny would spot me. He hadn't seen me in over a year. I figured that all faces must come to look alike to these guys after a while, especially to a singer like Johnny, who always seemed to be trying to communicate with somebody who wasn't there. But then damn, right in the middle of his second number those big eyes rested smack on me, and he saw right through the blond hair. If anything, those eyes got even bigger, filling up with fright and astonishment. He kept singing but I don't think he heard himself. Those big peepers stayed fixed on me for about thirty seconds. I smiled softly at him. Then he looked away and for the next twenty minutes or so pointedly ignored me.

After the show I headed for his dressing room, which was dumb, because it was obvious from his reaction that he knew a little something of what was happening with me. I should have left him alone, but I wanted to see a familiar face again; and anyway, I felt I could trust him. He didn't seem the type to rush to a telephone to call Somebody.

When I knocked on his door backstage he didn't answer.

"Johnny?" I called.

No answer.

I opened the door. He was sitting in a chair, his back to his makeup mirror, which was framed in very bright, glaring bulbs. This backdrop made him appear positively devilish, but the expression in his face wasn't hostile or unfriendly, just sort of guarded.

"May I come in?"

He didn't say anything, so I closed the door behind me and stood there with a big smile.

"You were magnificent," I said.

"You must be out of your mind," he whispered. "What are you doing here?"

"I just wanted to come by and say hello."

"I don't mean *here*, I mean in this town. Are you insane?"

I shrugged. "I got lonely," I said.

"Lock the door for Christ's sake."

I did that.

He shook his head and sighed.

"I'm sorry, Johnny," I said. "I don't want to get anybody in trouble."

"You're bad news, Terry," he said. "In headlines."

"I just wanted to see *somebody*."

"Why me?" he asked sadly.

"It's still a free country, Johnny, for Christ's sake."

"Maybe the country; not everybody in it necessarily."

The poor guy. He was in Charley's bag, one way or another, the same as I had been. I was the bad apple who'd rolled out, capable of contaminating from a distance. I sat down. He looked at me as if I'd just told him I'd seen his mother blowing a babboon or something.

"I know they're looking for me," I said quietly. "But I'm tired of running."

"Why me?"

"I don't know anybody else here. Anyway, I know I can trust you."

He didn't seem to appreciate the fact. He closed his eyes and sighed again.

"I owe Charley a lot, Terry," he said.

"How much?" I asked warily.

"Don't worry. Not *that* much. I don't owe anybody that much, thank God."

"Thanks, Johnny."

"Somebody was around a week ago, but I think it's okay now. But don't bet on it."

"Christ, Johnny, I don't even know what I did."

He grunted. "You didn't do anything. It was done to you. You talked to the police."

"Hell, not voluntarily; they picked me up. All I said was hello and goodbye. I couldn't tell them anything because I didn't *know* anything."

"Charley couldn't be sure of that," he said. "And anyway what got him was them telling you what he did for a living. He worries a lot about that. He didn't want them picking you up again and you telling them things without even realizing it. These people don't take chances, Terry."

"So I've learned."

"I don't know how you're still alive."

"You heard about what happened, huh?"

"Everybody knows," he said. "Four men are dead. You've got more lives than a cat."

"Plus the money."

"I don't want to know about that. Don't tell me anything about the money."

"I'm tired of running, Johnny. I'm tired of being afraid. It's crazy, the whole thing. I didn't do anything wrong and they're trying to wipe me out. I can't go to the police because I don't know who's in Charley's pocket."

"So you come to this town. Why don't you just go and knock on his front door?"

"I'm afraid of his wife," I said sarcastically. "She's a lesbian."

"They've got to live too," he muttered.

I wondered about him. I always had the feeling he was queer, or at least not particularly hot for the girls. Can you be a little bit queer? Christ, who cared? He was a guy I was taking advantage of and who was trying to be kind.

"Where are you staying?"

I told him, then wondered if I should have. He read my mind.

"Don't worry, Terry," he said, as if insulted.

"I'm not Terry here. I'm Audrey DeLand."

"Well, whoever you are, they'll find you soon enough without my help."

"Thanks for the encouragement."

"How long are you planning to stay in town?"

"I don't know."

"Get out now."

"You said it's safe."

"For God's sake, they don't tell me everything, you know. There could be two cannons outside the door right now, for all I know."

"Where can I go, Johnny?"

"Don't ask me. If I knew I'd go there myself."

No wonder he sang those teary ballads so beautifully; he was an unhappy guy.

"Those lousy cops," I said. "They set me up."

He gave me a wise-old-owl look. "Terry, if it wasn't that, it would have been something else. How long do you think it lasts?"

"I thought it would last forever," I said ruefully.

"Forever, huh? You're living on borrowed time now." He lowered his head and ran his fingers through his thick blond hair.

"I'm going to make it, Johnny," I said. "You'll see. I'll come through."

He looked up at me with a little smile. He didn't believe it.

"You'll see," I said.

"I hope so, Terry," he said quietly.

"Do you think if I gave back the money..."

"Don't ask me that," he said, suddenly angry. "Don't ask me those things, Terry. For God's sake."

"I'm sorry, Johnny," I said. "I don't want to involve you."

"Then keep away."

He lowered his head again and sulked, his fingers clenched in his hair. Now and then he shook his head disgustedly from side to side. I got the feeling it was the world rather than me he was thinking about. Then he said quietly, without looking up, "To answer your question ... no ... it wouldn't make any difference. He wants you on a slab. Period."

There followed about five minutes of unhappy silence. Then he said, without looking up, "Be careful when you leave."

Chapter Twenty

Believe it or not, I felt a little better when I left Johnny. Because I found myself feeling sorry for him, sorrier than for myself. He had been caught up by Charley somehow and couldn't fight back. At least I was out there defending my rights, saying screw you to the bullies. After talking to Johnny I was more determined than ever to stay alive, and to do it my way. They had no right to own people and push them around like that. They took away a person's self-respect and dignity. I don't know how much dignity I had, or ever had, but I sure as hell had my self-respect. If it had to cost me, then I'd pay the price.

I went into the hotel coffee shop for a late-night snack before going upstairs. The place was almost empty. I couldn't help noticing a guy sitting at a nearby table. He was a solidly put together guy, with black curly hair and a face that was interesting in a handsomely rugged sort of way. He was wearing a dark suit, which didn't look right on him—suits plainly weren't his style; he should have been wearing a plaid shirt and jeans, because the image he conveyed unquestionably was an outdoors one. He was sitting over a cup of coffee that you knew was cold now and which he probably hadn't tasted even once. He had the Las Vegas stare, that thousand-mile glazed stare which meant only one thing in this town.

He looked over at me, caught me staring, and he smiled, sort of sheepishly, as if he knew that I knew.

"You can't win them all," he said across two empty tables, sounding more like a philosopher than an unhappy loser.

"Who says?"

"Law of averages. Far as I know, it's never been repealed."

"You look like you could use some company," I said, knowing I sounded just like a hooker. But tell me, given the codes we've come to accept in this society, is it possible for a woman to invite a man over to her table and not sound like a hooker? Especially in Las Vegas at one o'clock in the morning? And I wasn't exactly dressed like Mother Superior.

He pushed his chair back, got up, walked slowly over, and sat down opposite me, tilting his head slightly to a side and watching me with an expression of faintly amused expectancy.

"You look like your luck's run out on you," I said.

"Clean out," he said with a slow, good-natured, what-the-hell grin. His white shirt was open at the collar; his tie had been folded over several times and tucked neatly into his jacket pocket. He had a nice face, with strong masculine lines that suggested kindness and understanding.

"You look mighty uncomfortable in that suit," I said, realizing as soon as I said it that that was another hooker-sounding line.

"Little lady," he said, "I am mighty uncomfortable in this whole town. Too many lights, too many people, too many sidewalks."

"Where are you from?"

"Junction Waters," he said, as though he were saying New York or Chicago or San Francisco or someplace that you could immediately identify in your head. He read the blank look in my face. "Snake River country," he said.

"That really clears it up," I said.

He shook his head and laughed, at himself. "Pardon me," he said. "You know how it is with your home town—you're so familiar with it you think the rest of the world must know it too. Junction Waters is up in Idaho."

"I never met anybody from Idaho before."

"Aren't too many people there to meet. Idaho's still a big secret and we want to keep it that way."

"You a farmer?" I asked.

"I've got a little patch of land. Mostly I raise snow, it seems," he said with a big hearty laugh. You couldn't help but join in when he laughed—his laughter had that quality.

"What's your name?" I asked.

"Dwight Douglas," he said. "I was named after Eisenhower—the general, not the president."

"I thought they were the same man," I said.

"Not to my father. I was born on D-Day in 1944, you see, when Ike was the general. My father was a red-hot Democrat all his life; he was sorry for the name after Ike became a Republican and was elected president. So everybody calls me 'Doug'—except my Republican friends," he added with a laugh. "What about you?" he asked. "What's your name?"

"Terry," I said, before I even realized it. It sounded strange—my own name sounded strange to me. Hell, I hadn't used it in weeks. But for some reason I found myself not wanting to lie to this guy.

"Sexy name," he said with a wink.

"I'll bet you think I'm a hooker, the way I invited you over."

"Oh, no. These Vegas hookers can spot empty pockets; I think they've got X-ray eyes."

"You went to the cleaners, huh?"

"At the tables. Boy, did I. And I wasn't trying to break the bank either. Just trying to clear expenses and show a modest profit. Then I was just trying to catch up and go home even. Then I was rolling for gas money." He shook his head and grunted a little laugh. "Dee-saster and devastation," he said. "Whenever I picked up those dice and shook them near my ear I didn't hear rattling, I heard them whispering, 'Fuck you.' Pardon the profanity. But I was totaled."

"How much did you lose?"

"Four thousand dollars."

"What brought you down to Vegas?"

"I'd never been here, heard so much about it and thought I'd take a chance. When I came down here I honestly thought I had a chance to win. I wanted to pick up about six thousand, that's all. You see, I've got an option on some land up at Junction Waters that I can get for a

175

good price. The six thousand would have been the down payment. Well, that's gone. Goodbye to opportunity."

"That's too bad."

"Serves me right. But I've got no complaints. Made my own decision, and nobody cheated me."

"You're not bitter?"

"When you've got only yourself to be mad at, it's hard to be bitter. What are you doing in town?"

"Just traveling," I said.

"Where's your home?"

"Nowhere."

He frowned, giving me a very penetrating look. Then he smiled and nodded. "Okay," he said quietly, understandingly.

"I hate sounding mysterious."

"Your privilege."

"The thing is," I said, "I'm trying to make a new life for myself."

"That's hard as hell," he said, "if you don't mind my telling you. Unless you've had some disastrous experiences, of course. And I don't mean blowing your money at the crap table; I mean, some real serious stuff. Like when I was in Vietnam, for instance. Now there, under those circumstances, I saw some guys' whole personalities and outlooks and everything undergo vast change. When those guys got home, they were going to make new lives for themselves, because of what they experienced. It takes something like that."

"Shock," I said.

"You could call it that," he said. "But you can't just say that it's going to be a new life unless the person inside changes. And it takes one hell of a lot to compel that. I mean, something's got to reach *deep inside* you."

"The shock of losing your money didn't do that to you?"

"Money? Ah, hell, no. In a few years I'll work that bankroll up again. Anyway, I didn't start out from discontent. I was happy when I got here, I'll be happy when I leave—more or less."

"When are you leaving?"

"Somebody told me there's something called Travelers Aid or some such that will lend you some money to get home on. I don't need much, just gas money, and maybe enough for a night's lodging. I'll look them up tomorrow."

"Listen," I said, "will you do me a favor?"

"If I can."

"No questions asked?"

"Can't promise that," he said.

"I've got a lot of money and I want to give you some."

He stared at me, his eyes narrowing.

"Will you take it?" I asked.

"Why should you want to do that?"

"Because you seem like a nice guy."

He leaned back in his chair and put a hand on his chin. I felt a little twinge of guilt—without ever expecting to, I had thrown a problem into this guy's lap. Instead of grabbing for the money, he wanted to think about it first.

"I don't know, little lady," he said. "You know, the world just isn't built that way, one stranger offering another money."

"It can happen, Doug," I said. "It *is* happening. With no strings attached."

He forced a little laugh that made his shoulders shrug.

"I suppose this world is crazy enough for anything to happen. But why should it happen to me?"

"Because you're lucky," I said.

"You wouldn't have said that an hour ago."

"Will you take it?"

"How much?"

I looked in my bag. There was a thick packet of fifties in there.

"Around four or five thousand," I said.

"I thought you were going to say fifty dollars."

I took the money out, wrapped it in a paper napkin, and pushed it across the table at him. He regarded it thoughtfully.

"I don't understand this at all," he said.

"Come on. Pick it up and go away."

"Go where?"

"Anywhere you want. Home. Back to the tables."

177

"Did you win that?"

"I don't gamble," I said.

"Neither do I, normally. Listen, I can't take your money."

"You're being foolish."

"I've been being foolish since I pulled in."

"If you don't take that money," I said, "you're going to drive home tomorrow and spend the rest of your life wondering what might have happened."

"All the same . . ."

"Look, if I had offered you fifty dollars to get home on, you would have taken it, right?"

"Probably."

"So the difference is in the amount, right? Listen, what's so holy and sacred about money? It's mine and I want to give it to you. If you want to turn around and give it to a guy selling pencils on the corner, then it's your business. So take it. Come on, take it. If you don't, I'm going to start yelling 'Rape!' "

"This is the damnedest thing," he said.

Since he didn't seem able to make up his mind, I did it for him. I simply got up and walked out of there without looking back.

Chapter Twenty-one

When I woke up the next morning I was thinking about Doug, wondering what he had done. Did he pick up the money and go home or go right back to the tables? I didn't know, but I felt good. But what the hell was I trying to do?—perform a string of good deeds hoping that would get me in heaven? Christ, I didn't know. Maybe Charley would find out that I gave away thousands of dollars of his money to a waitress and to some unlucky Idaho cowboy and he would think what a good-hearted Jane I was and call off his dogs. Sure. Keep pouring it out, Terry, until some winged creature comes down from the clouds, drapes you in a bulletproof Dior gown, and says to the world, "Thou shalt not harm this benevolent child." Bullshit, Terry. The way to stay alive was to keep a grip on those dollars; they were all I had to keep me bouncing along in this lethal game of checkers.

I had breakfast in the hotel coffee shop, then went out for a walk. It was a hot day, close to ninety, with a warm breeze blowing in off the desert. You see a lot of bleary faces on the street in Vegas in the morning and you never know whether they belong to people who have just got up or who are trying to find their way to bed after outlasting the night.

I wandered in and out of the hotels, drinking coffee, watching the action in the casinos, ignoring the inquiring eyes of the men. I felt cold about sex at the moment; I don't know why. Maybe I was just being defensive; Christ, in this town you couldn't be sure whom to trust. It would be just hell to go up to the room with a guy, get undressed, and find myself facing a .38 instead of a roaring hard-on. Most of my life I'd gone along hoping to meet men. I'd always enjoyed their company; but all of a sudden I found myself wary of them. Once upon a time I would never have thought twice about letting myself be picked up by a guy whose looks I liked. Now now. Not this day, anyway.

That's probably why I didn't mind when Angel sat down next to me. I was sitting in the lobby of a plush, air-conditioned hotel on the Strip, people-watching. I enjoyed doing that; it can be fun, especially in a place like Vegas, with the characters that you see there. I watched the hustlers, the sharpies, the fat cats with their trim and pampered little nymphs (some of them no longer so nymphie), the tourists, the Mom and Pop bus tour people, the conventioneers with their florid faces and loud jokes. An endless parade. I felt secure behind my shades; they didn't look conspicuous because I was getting the feeling that every other person in Vegas wore them.

"Oh, dear," she said, plunking herself down next to me on the sofa. "My feet. There ought to be a law against high heels, don't you think? Especially on hot days on concrete sidewalks."

This was Angel. That was her name. Angel McBride. She didn't look much like an angel. She was about thirty-five, had a little butch haircut, sort of a plain face with a nice smile, though her eyes were cagey, doing a lot of winkless staring when she looked at you. She was wearing a dowdy red dress—the Main Street special back home, I guess ("You'll wow 'em in Vegas with that, honey.")—with an orchid pinned up over her little bosom. She had good legs though and solid thighs, neither of which she seemed shy about showing when she crossed them.

"Can I bum a cigarette?" she said.

"I've given them up," I said.

"Lucky you. I'll never have that discipline."

She was in town for a bookkeepers' convention, she said. She was from Iowa and her boss insisted she go, for a combination vacation, "whoopee time," and business.

"I think he feels sorry for me," she said. "Most men do, for a woman my age who's not married. They think we never have fun. I'd hate to tell him," she said with a wink, then laughed, leaning over and touching me on the arm for a moment.

"I'm head bookkeeper, you see," she said after she'd sent a bellboy for a pack of butts and was puffing away. "He sent me down here because we're supposed to be hearing lectures about streamlining procedures and saving the company money. Frankly, I think it's a lot of crap. But I guess I'm enjoying myself."

She was a chatterbox, going on about her job, her boss, the plane ride, the people she'd met. I just sat and listened. I found it nice to be talking with a woman for a change. In fact it seemed almost a novelty. It occurred to me how little time I'd spent in the company of women the past few years. I used to enjoy those gossipy bull sessions with the girls in those long-ago days when I was a job-holder. You just can't gossip with a man the same way.

Next thing I knew I was in a candlelit lounge having drinks with Angel McBride. She wouldn't let me buy, saying she was on the expense account for the first time in her life, and was learning fast how to use it.

"I'll put you down as Miss Jones, head bookkeeper of an importing firm in San Francisco," she said as we lifted snifters of brandy. "And we discussed credits and debits."

"Whoever they are," I said as we both laughed. She had a funny way of laughing; it sounded fine but her eyes brightened when she laughed and focused right on you and never blinked. Wide unblinking eyes and a laughing mouth make you look like a looney. But stop being so criticial, Terry, I told myself. That's just the way she is. Christ, maybe it was the brandies, but I felt myself more relaxed than I'd been in a long time.

She didn't ask me too many questions about myself, for which I was grateful. I was tired of making up stories. She did ask where I was from and I said Chicago and in my giddiness told her I ran a massage parlor. She looked startled for a moment, as if she believed it, until I told her it was called "Banger's Trust," and then she laughed out loud and said, "Oh, go on."

Then, after about five brandies apiece she became serious and began talking about her life. It was sort of a sad story. She'd fallen in love with a married man in her town and they'd carried on for two years, with the guy making the usual promises of getting a divorce. Which he never did, of course, and probably never had any intention of ever doing. She became disillusioned, ate a lot of sweets to smother her unhappiness, ballooned up to 240 pounds, and then fought her way back down. She lived with her mother now and apparently it wasn't a fun life. It was all very sad and she sat looking into the candle on the table as if seeing the rest of her life there, burning away in a narrow flame inside of a glass bell.

Then she was looking me full in the eyes, with that strange piercing gaze she had, made even stranger by the candlelight, like she was trying to hypnotize.

"I'm staying right across the street," she said. "Why don't we go up to my room and have a drink there?"

Oh-oh. All those little signals started flashing inside my head. Sobriety, come to the rescue. Jeez, who needed this? I thought again of Helene Corbett. Up until that time I'd been kind of liberal about the oddies: live and let live. But that had changed my mind. Of course I'd been raped—no two ways about it. If it hadn't been for that I might have gone with Angel McBride, just for the hell of it. A different experience. That sort of thing. I mean, I wasn't *morally* against it, it was just that the experience with Helene had been so awful, it had soured me. All the same, I was tempted. I was sorely in need of some close companionship, some tenderness. And I was sure that under the right circumstances a little fling with a lesbian might be fun. Surrender myself to a woman, swoon into it.

But no. I just couldn't. Helene had ruined it for me. I'd heard about women turning frigid against all men after having been raped by one, and I supposed it went the same way with being raped by a woman.

But I didn't want Angel to know what I was thinking. I couldn't just come out and say, no, I don't swing that way. I didn't want to embarrass her. And I don't think I was misinterpreting anything, either; there was no question in my mind what she wanted. It was in her eyes, the desire and the offer, the question. That steady gaze was full of loneliness and passion.

"Just one drink," she said, smiling, her face softening now.

I felt embarrassed, as if she had read my mind.

"I'll take a raincheck," I said, as sincerely as I could. "When are you going home?"

"The day after tomorrow."

"Well, there's time then."

"To tell you the truth, Florence," (that was the name I'd given her; I'd forgotten my Vegas name) "you're the first person I've dared to talk to outside of the meeting rooms." She gave a giggle. "I thought I'd have a wild old scandalous time in Las Vegas, but I found myself just too inhibited for it."

"You ought to travel more often," I said.

"Maybe," she said. "But I'll tell you what. Why don't I play hooky from the convention tomorrow morning and rent a car and we can take a drive out to the desert? Everyone says it's beautiful and should be seen."

"That sounds like a good idea," I said.

"Why don't I pick you up outside your hotel at nine o'clock?"

"Make it ten," I said.

I ate dinner by myself, went to a show, then went back to my room. A drive in the desert with lonely Angel McBride. What the hell. Maybe I'd ask her if there were any job openings in her little town in Iowa and go back with her and settle into anonymous respectability. I used to be a first-rate typist. Sure. Go back to it. God, what a thought. I laughed at it while soaping myself up in the shower.

Suppose she made a pass at me out on the desert? Oh, shit, Terry, I told myself, stop worrying about it. If she started sending out the signals again I'd just start talking about men, about big strong balls and huge plunging peckers. That would turn her off. At least she was somebody to talk to. I hadn't realized how much I'd been missing that. I'd really enjoyed the time I spent with her. I'd enjoyed talking to a frustrated little lezzie bookkeeper from Iowa. Boy, I was probably in rougher shape than I imagined. With all of those sun-tanned hunks of masculine splendor parading around, I'd settled for brandy with Angel McBride. Oh, well.

I'd just stepped out of the shower wrapped in a bath towel when the phone rang. I stared at it for a moment. Who the hell was *that*? Angel McBride? She didn't know what name I'd registered under. (Hell, I'd forgotten myself what name I'd registered under.) I let it ring five times, then couldn't bear it any longer and picked it up. I was scared. I was shaking.

"Hello?"

"Terry?"

"Who is this?"

"Johnny Blake." He was whispering; he sounded scared. Two scared people talking to each other.

"What do you want?"

"Get out of town. I just heard this. There's a gun in town looking for you."

Oh, Christ.

"Who is it, Johnny?" I asked.

"I have no idea."

"What does he look like?"

He paused. I heard him expel a breath.

"It isn't a man," he said. "It's a woman."

Then he hung up.

Chapter Twenty-two

I don't think I slept a wink all night. Maybe I did and maybe I didn't, because I don't know; I don't remember. I don't remember anything about that night except that my body became stiff as a board and I was afraid to move in bed, as if all of Las Vegas had me wired for sound.

It's bad enough to know they're after you; but if you can keep one step ahead of them it's all right, because that determination and the frantic pace keeps you on sort of a high and you can tolerate a hell of a lot. But when all of a sudden you hear that one of them has slipped into town ... that somewhere near there's a living, breathing human being whose sole purpose in life at the moment is to put you into your grave, you begin to feel you're living a screaming nightmare. They say the mind can adjust to anything, and that must be true, because I'd forgotten how horrible the death threat was. Well, it all came back to me that night. God, more than anything else it was the *aloneness*: a whole goddamned teeming crazy city out there and nobody really giving a damn (except maybe Johnny Blake a little bit; enough to warn me, anyway).

And then to hear it was a woman. That made it even weirder. A woman on the trigger? I'd never heard of that before. It was awful to have to be wary of every man you met, but now every woman too?

Angel McBride? Don't think I didn't give her one hell of a lot of thought. But she couldn't be the one; it was impossible. She was just a little bookkeeper from Iowa—or else she was the world's greatest actress. No, not her; she was just a horny lezzie who wanted to take a dive into me. They would never try to set me up with a broad like that. No, it would have to be some swinging, with-it type, since that was more my style. Or was it? Christ, I had sat for hours with Angel McBride and had been half tempted to go upstairs with her, hadn't I? Maybe they knew me better than I knew myself. What a scary, depressing thought.

Well, there was only one thing to do: get out of town. But to where? That question was coming up with more and more frequency. Hell, I didn't *know* where. I'd just go out to the airport and listen to what departures they were announcing, pick one out and go.

I got out of bed the next morning almost drugged with depressed unhappiness. Again I left my wardrobe behind, going out with just the clothes on my back and the bag of money. The room was paid up in advance so I didn't have to worry about stiffing the hotel. I just wanted out of there as fast as possible.

When I stepped into the corridor I almost had a heart attack. There was a woman there, a goddamned amazon, about six feet tall, shapely though a bit heavy in the ass. She was wearing shades and a big, floppy-brimmed hat. She didn't look like she was doing anything in particular out there, just sort of wandering around. She was about twenty feet away. I slammed the door behind me and was immediately sorry—I hadn't taken the room key with me. I was stuck out there with her. I stared at her and she came walking slowly toward me. She was carrying a big white handbag.

I didn't know what to do. What the hell *do* you do in a situation like that, where you're not sure? How do you go about trying to save your life and at the same time not make a fool of yourself? But then the decision was taken out of my hands, when a door opened and a young couple came out. They looked like honeymooners, the way they were holding hands and she was gazing up at him.

"Good morning," I said to them cheerily.

"Hi," they said.

I walked with them to the elevator and the guy pressed the button. The amazon kept coming, moving up behind me and then stopping to wait for the elevator too. I shut my eyes for a moment. She wouldn't do it there, would she? In front of two witnesses? Or would she do all three of us? I opened my eyes and watched the little light pop onto one floor number after another over my head. Behind

186

the door I could hear the elevator motoring up. It finally came to a stop at our floor and the doors opened. We all stepped in. The doors came together and the elevator began to descend.

I had positioned myself as far from the amazon as I could, watching her out of the corner of my eye. She seemed very cool and self-possessed. Christ, if she was the one, how the hell had she found me? Maybe they'd got to poor Johnny Blake and worked him over; or maybe Johnny had blown the whistle without any encouragement, to try and win a few points with Charley.

Well, I wasn't murdered in the elevator. When the doors opened to the lobby I realized I'd been holding my breath and let it out in a rush. I hurried across the lobby, holding firmly to my bag of money, heading for the revolving doors. She was right behind me—I could see her reflection in the spinning glass doors. When I stepped outside into the glaring morning sun I was beginning to feel panic. Christ, she was big and seemed to be getting bigger by the minute, and spooky, too, with those shades and that hat with the big floppy brim. I didn't know what to do. If I took a cab, so would she. If I went to the airport, so would she. If I got on a plane all she had to do was see which one, where it was going, and telephone Charley, who would then rush a couple of gunnies to meet me at the other end.

Then I heard somebody calling, "Hey! Hey!" I looked and there was Angel McBride, having pulled right up in front of the hotel. Now I knew why they called her Angel. I gave her a big smile and got in next to her and closed the door. I watched the amazon as we pulled away; she was looking back at me. I stuck my tongue out at her, which gave her a start because she suddenly threw back her shoulders and straightened up.

"Right on time," Angel said cheerfully.

"Really?" I asked. I hadn't been paying the slightest attention to time.

"Had breakfast?" she asked.

"No."

"Well, I inquired this morning, and there's a little

187

restaurant about thirty miles out on the desert which everybody recommends. By everybody I mean the desk clerk in my hotel," she added with a laugh.

"Good," I said. "I feel like getting out of town this morning." Far, far out, I told myself.

"You look like you've packed your own lunch."

"What? Oh, the bag. I brought a bathing suit and a change of clothes in case we decide to go swimming later." Jeez, I was becoming a good liar—quick, creative, and uninhibited.

She glanced at me with a faint smile. Shit, I thought, why did she have to be that way? I could just feel that twisted little corner of her mind working: swimming, changing clothes together in some goddamned locker or somewhere. But sorry, baby, there was hardly a bathing suit and towel in this bag, and buddy or not, your nose ain't getting nowhere near my garden of glory. I was sorry to disappoint her, but at least let her enjoy thinking about it.

She chattered on steadily as we drove away from the city out onto the flat, dull desert. Up ahead the heat was shimmering on the highway, but inside the car it was air-conditioned and comfortable. I was wondering how I was going to convince her later on to drive me to the airport, and how I was going to explain the "sudden" decision. I could tell her that I had to meet a friend. That was a pretty good idea, I thought. Once we got out there I could lose her and get on a goddamned plane and go somewhere.

I sat back and watched the desert scenery pass. Not the most exciting thing I'd ever seen, but it *was* different. Then I became aware that she had stopped talking and that we were going faster. I looked at Angel. She was constantly glancing into the rear-view mirror.

"What's the matter?" I asked.

She frowned. "I think we're being followed."

I whirled around in the seat. Sure enough, there was another car, pretty far behind us.

"How do you know they're following us?" I asked. This was a straight-ass highway, with no other roads around it; that other car had no choice but to follow.

"A hunch," she said, watching the mirror.

If we were being followed, and I still wasn't sure that we were, then it could only be Charley's gun-baby—probably the amazon from the hotel. Suddenly I felt sorry for poor Angel. She had gotten herself into the middle of a nasty situation. Maybe I ought to tell her what was going on. I considered it, but then decided against, on two counts: one, she was apt to shit right in her pants and do something fatally foolish; and two, I still wasn't sure that we really were being followed. If it turned out that we were, then I was going to have to tell her what the situation was, because I was going to need her help.

"We'll see," she muttered, glancing again into the mirror and suddenly accelerating. That desert began to fly by so fast the roadside brush was like a blur. We were riding in a compact and when that thing got over eighty it began to shake and rattle.

"Take it easy, huh?" I said.

"They're following," she said angrily. "They've accelerated."

"Who do you think it is?" I asked.

"You tell me," she said, flashing me a hot-eyed look. "Who the hell do you know in Vegas who would be following us out here? Who the hell were you talking to?"

Oh, my God, I moaned, squeezing my eyes shut for a second. This was Charley's gunnie, this bullshit teller, and I was sitting in a car with her going ninety miles an hour.

"You'd better stop and let me out right now," I said. "That's the police behind us."

"Horseshit," she said, picking up her little handbag which had been lying between us on the seat and putting it on her lap. I knew why she did that, because I knew what she had in that bag.

I turned around; whoever was behind us either wasn't following or else was losing heart: that other car was getting smaller and smaller.

"Just sit back and shut your mouth," she said.

"You phony son of a bitch," I said. "Bookkeeper. Iowa. What a line of crap."

"Shut up."

"I'll bet you're a goddamn dyke, though," I said. "I bet that part of it's true."

"I told you to shut up," she said angrily.

"Has Charley fed you to his wife yet?" I asked, yelling.

Now she turned beet red and glared at me, grimacing so her lower teeth were bared. I guess I'd touched a nerve.

"You're sick, all of you!" I cried. "All a bunch of freaked-out perverts!"

She swung out and hit me in the face with the back of her hand, a real shot. But I guess you shouldn't do that at ninety miles an hour, because before she could get that hand back to the wheel she had lost control. She panicked. So did I. The car crossed the white line—there was nobody coming in the other direction, luckily—and she fought to get it straightened out. But she twisted the wheel too suddenly and too sharply and we shot right off of the road, bounced over a low embankment and tore into the desert, throwing up clouds of dust on all sides. The car bounded and rattled like it was trying to tear itself apart, and I remembered in a fleeting but vivid thought going off the road with Big Stoney and Mac; it was happening again. Christ, I was living my life over again, as that car was grinding forward, the rocks flying up underneath and clunking against it.

Then I guess she was hitting the brakes, because all of a sudden we started to swerve in what seemed like two different directions at once, still going at a terrific speed, and then we pitched over and thudded to a savagely abrupt halt. I was hanging by my seat belt—we had tipped over on the driver's side. God almighty, I'd done this before too, having to hoist myself out through the window. But this time I was going to have to do it in a hurry because I smelled smoke. I got the window down, unbuckled the belt, and raised myself out of there. I dropped from the car to the ground and began running like crazy. I looked back once and the smoke was pouring out from the bottom of the car, and I saw a few quick little tongues of fire. Jesus, I thought, she was still in there, though in what condition I didn't know—unconscious or maybe even dead,

190

since she never made a sound after the car turned over. Either way, I was damned if I was going back.

As I ran toward the highway I saw the other car just pulling up. Then I heard the explosion. The sound of it knocked me stumbling and I pitched face forward into the desert sands.

We were still going at sunset. I wouldn't let him stop; just once for gas, that was all. I told him if he stopped for any other reason I would have a stroke. So we kept going. After I'd told him that the person in the car had been trying to kill me he didn't ask any questions. He fell silent for a long while, thinking about it, I guess, because he said, "You'll have to tell me about it sometime."

"Sometime," I said.

We just kept heading north. Route 15. I kept seeing those signs. Out of Nevada, through the northwesternmost corner of Arizona and on into Utah. We passed Zion National Park, then Fishlake National Forest, on up to Salt Lake City, and right on past it. Daylight started to fade in northern Utah and I was starving and knew he must be too, but I still wouldn't let him stop. Only for gas.

Sometimes he was quiet, sometimes he talked. He'd seen us leaving Vegas and had indeed been following. He wanted to see me again. For a long while I wasn't paying close attention, but then it started coming through. He'd taken the money and gone back to the tables, after sitting for almost two hours deciding if that was what he wanted to do. Then he figured the hell with it, and went back inside and he got hot. He stayed hot for three hours and when he started to cool off he took a break. "That's the smart way," he said. "Let 'em heat up again." He went back after an hour and sure enough, the dice had warmed up again for him.

"I told myself when I reached fifty thousand I'd stop," he said. "And that's what I did. Walked away in the middle of a roll and cashed in. Thanks to you, little lady. All thanks to you. Sold my shebang and bought this baby for five thousand cash—what do you think about that air-conditioning? The shebang didn't have air in it and I sweated like a pig driving down. Not anymore. And say, listen, I owe it all to you."

Fifty thousand. He'd made fifty thousand. I didn't have the heart to tell him that about nine times fifty thousand had gone up in smoke with that murderous little bitch back there. But I didn't care. That wasn't real money anyway. Never was. Charley would give up now. He would have to. That was five of his people dead. And even if he didn't, let him look. Let him send his whole goddamned army out looking. They'd go to Miami and L.A. and New York and Nassau and Acapulco and probably Honolulu and Rio too. Charley thought he knew me. Well, he didn't. He'd never look for me in . . . where was it again?

"Snake River country," Doug said proudly.

"Tell me about it," I said.

"Ah," he said with deep feeling. "It winds around the Grand Tetons. There's places where you can see the forests and the snow-topped peaks in the river. And you'll see eagles and osprey, and you'll see moose grazing, and the prettiest green meadow lands dotted with beaver ponds. The flowers blaze in June and July and August, and then the snow comes. Tons of it. Seems like it'll never stop, never go away. But it does. You get used to it. Some people think winter's the best time up there. It gets soooo quiet."

"Quiet?" I said.

"You'll hear a snowflake drop."

"I love that sound," I said. I snuggled in against him. He put one big strong arm around me. "What's the best time for making love up there?" I asked.

"Winter's great for that," he said with a laugh. "Not much else to do then. Spring is great too because of the inspiration that's on the air. Summer makes it sweet. Some people think fall is best though, because of the tang in the air. The tang cools the summer blood and brings on a whole new set of inspirations."

"Get me there," I said.

"I'm gettin'," he said. Then he started to sing a country-western song. He had a nice voice, too.